SKELETON KEYS

THE UNIMAGINARY FRIEND

For Ruth, of course! ~ Guy Bass

For Cath and Leni ~ Pete Williamson

STRIPES PUBLISHING LIMITED

An imprint of the Little Tiger Group
1 Coda Studios, 189 Munster Road,
London SW6 6AW

A paperback original
First published in Great Britain in 2019

ISBN: 978-1-78895-030-5

A CIP catalogue record for this book is available
from the British Library.

Printed and bound in the UK.

2 4 6 8 10 9 7 5 3 1

SKELETON KEYS

KEYS

THE UNIMAGINARY FRIEND

WRITTEN BY
GUY BASS

ILLUSTRATED BY
PETE WILLIAMSON

The Key to
Reality

The Key to
Second Sight

The Key to
Doorminion

The Forbidden Key

The Key to Time

The Key to
Possibility

The Key to
a Quick Getaway

The Key to
the Kingdom

The Key to Imagination

The Key to Oblivion

Greetings! To dallywanglers, ringdingers and snuggabouts! To the imaginary and the unimaginary! To the living, the dead and everyone in between, my name is Keys ... Skeleton Keys.

Many moons ago, I began my existence as an IF – an imaginary friend. Then, one day, I suddenly became as real as kneecaps! I had become what we in the business of imagining call *unimaginary*.

But I am more than just a handsome bag o' bones. For these fantabulant fingers of mine can open doors to hidden worlds and secret places ... doors to the limitless realm of all the imagination.

Ol' Mr Keys has seen all there is worth hearing, heard everything there is to see and forgotten more stories than I shall ever remember. Oh, the things I know would curl your toes! The stories I could tell you...

But of course *stories* are why you are here.
Well, have I got a hum-dum-dinger for you,
set to blow your mind out of your nose-holes.
This unimaginary tale is so truly unbelievable
that it must, unbelievably, be true.

Meet Ben Bunsen. Now,
I know what you are
thinking – why should
I care a jot about this
little ankle-sprout? He
may have a head and
toes and soul as any
person might possess,
but he is certainly no
dashing, key-fingered skeleton
with a thousand adventures
under his belt and a thousand
more to come! To look at
him, you might imagine he
is unremarkable – and, in

truth, most people would agree with you. Ben spends his days being ignored by other children. Why? He is not certain – for, if he was, he might attempt to do something about it.

As it is, Ben has only one friend in all the world. But since this is no ordinary tale, his is no ordinary friend. You see, the most remarkable thing about Ben's friend is that he is a figment of Ben's wild imagination. And strange things can happen when imaginations run wild...

Our story begins in a small town on a small island on the second Sunday of February. As mist rolls in over the ocean and the gulls caw in the darkening sky we see a higgledy-piggledy house – tall, crooked and but a stone's throw from a winding beach. It is Ben Bunsen's tenth birthday, and preparations are under way for a party to remember...

CHAPTER ONE

A SEA OF BALLOONS

(PARTY TIME)

"A little imagination goes a long way."
—SK

"How do I look?" Ben asked the Gorblimey. Since the Gorblimey was a figment of his imagination, there was no reply. All the same, Ben waited a moment and then said, "Thanks."

It was the first time Ben had ever had a birthday party. Invitations had been sent to almost every child on Grundy Island. Ben's mum and dad had spent all day getting the house ready. Multi-coloured balloons covered every inch of the floor ... bunting hung from the ceiling ... cakes, crisps, biscuits and a rainbow of fizzy drinks awaited the guests, not to mention gifts and games and an honest-to-goodness firework display in the garden. This was going to be a party to remember.

"One minute to go," he said, checking his watch. Ben had been in his bedroom in the attic of their higgledy-piggledy house for half an hour. His dad had suggested Ben wait there until everyone arrived, and then make "a big entrance" accompanied by cheering and party poppers.

Ben pressed his ear against the floor, trying in vain to listen for knocks at the door or the bustle of excited guests.

The seconds ticked away to half past three.

Party time.

"Wish me luck," Ben said. He ruffled his jet-black hair, which immediately fell back into its bowl-like shape. Then he straightened his very best jumper (the one with the big stripe, which his imaginary friend assured him brought out his eyes) and, with his heart thumping in his chest, he clambered down the ladder from his bedroom to the landing. The spiral staircase was all that stood between him and his first ever birthday party. Ben imagined the faces of his classmates waiting for him to appear. Cliff Pitchfork, the tallest boy in school ... Hattie Blanket, with her excellent laugh ... Ichabod Twist, who knew magic ... they had all found it easy to ignore him until now.

Ben often wondered why he had no friends. For as long as he could remember, Ben's dad had insisted that the family move house every year, relocating from one seaside town to another. Maybe that was the problem – maybe Ben knew his friendships could not last. Or maybe, he thought, he just wasn't the sort of person that *could* make friends.

Not real ones, at least.

But what if this was the day all that changed? What if one of his classmates actually wanted to be his friend? Or what if they *all* wanted to be his friend? Ben hardly dared to imagine it ... but imagine he did. He swelled with confidence as he made his way down the curling stairs and waded into a sea of balloons.

"I'm here," he said aloud. "I'm—"

Ben stopped. There, in the middle of the room, knee-deep in balloons with party hats perched on their heads, stood his mum and dad...

...and no one else.

For a moment Ben wondered if everyone was hiding. Perhaps his classmates were crouched behind sofas and chairs or hiding under balloons, ready to jump out and wish him a happy birthday. But then Ben's dad said:

"I'm so sorry, Benjy. But it doesn't look like anyone's going to make it."

Ben felt his thumping heart sink into the depths of his chest.

"N-no one came?" he muttered.

"I phoned around," said Ben's dad, rubbing the back of his head. "But no one answered."

"I'm sure they would have loved to come," added Ben's mum, trying to sound positive. "They're probably just ... busy."

Not for the first time, Ben pushed his feelings deep into the pit of his stomach. And he *imagined*.

"It ... it doesn't matter," he said softly.

"The Gorblimey's here."

"The who?" asked Ben's dad. "Oh, *him*."

Even though the Gorblimey was imaginary, Ben could picture him quite clearly – he was a sort of monster: hairy, round and as black as an eclipse, with kind, bright eyes, curved horns and a yellow-orange candle flame forever flickering in the air just above his head. The Gorblimey was loyal and kind and could shrink to fit in Ben's pocket and bounce right over a house and eat almost anything. And, most importantly, he was always there when Ben needed him.

"No, no, that won't do at all – this is a real party for real people!" Ben's dad continued. He urgently began gathering up balloons, horns and party poppers. "Come on, let's turn this into a door-to-door party!" he declared, stuffing handfuls of biscuits into his pockets. "Knock, knock! Who's there? Ben's birthday, that's who! We'll take Ben's birthday to every house on the island!"

"Bob, that's literally the worst idea you've ever had," tutted Ben's mum as Ben's dad blew loudly on a party horn. "*And* it was your idea to move us to this grotty little island."

"It's OK, really," said Ben, desperate to stop the inevitably humiliating door-to-door party before it started. "The Gorblimey's here. We can—"

"No!" Ben's dad suddenly interrupted. "This isn't a party for *imaginary* friends. You're ten now, Ben. You're too *old* for this sort of nonsense."

"Says the man who chooses to spend every free moment alone, building a boat out of matchsticks," noted Ben's mum.

"It's not a boat, it's a *ship* – and that's not the point," said Ben's dad. "Ben needs real friends."

"And one day I'm sure he'll make some but in the meantime he has his Gorblimey," insisted Ben's mum. "What harm can it do?"

"Look around," snapped Ben's dad. "If Ben didn't have imaginary friends, maybe the other children would have wanted to come to his party!"

That was too hard for Ben to hear. With tears in his eyes, he ran towards the front door in a flurry of flying balloons. Ben heard his dad cry, "I didn't mean— Wait!" but with a slam of the door, Ben was gone.

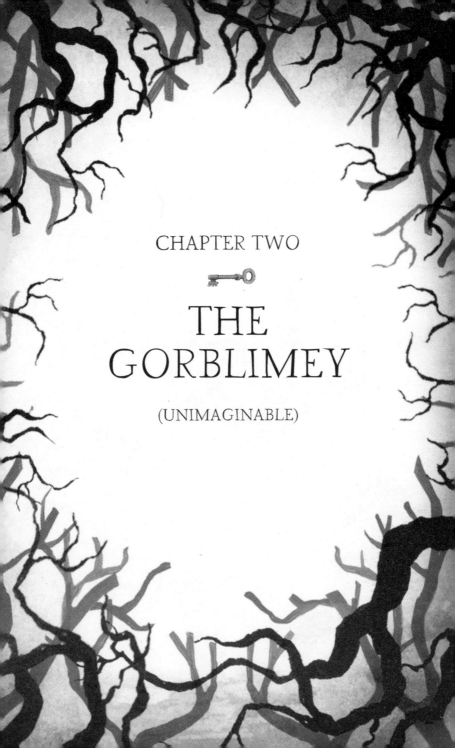

CHAPTER TWO

THE GORBLIMEY

(UNIMAGINABLE)

*"An IF is the creation
of a wild imagination!"*
—SK

B en ran outside into the cold, damp
fog and all the way down to the beach.
At the edge of the water he slumped into the
knee-soaking sand and stared out over the
sea.

Unlike his dad, who could spend hours
staring wistfully over any stretch of grey,
mist-laden water, Ben *hated* the ocean. It was
so huge that it always made him feel small
and alone. So Ben did what he always did
when he felt small and alone – he imagined
the Gorblimey was right there with him.

But this time, Ben screwed up his eyes and imagined harder than ever before. You could say he let his imagination run wild. For the first time, he imagined that the Gorblimey was *real*.

Ben opened his eyes ... and found himself still utterly alone. Not even the distant caw of a seagull could be heard. Ben stared at nothing, listened to the faint sound of waves lapping against his knees, and sighed.

Then, through the lazy, rolling fog, he noticed a dot of flickering light suddenly appear. It looked like a candle flame, hovering in the air, just above the glistening waves. Ben gazed at the light as it moved slowly towards him. He peered closer.

There was something in the water – a dark shape, just beneath the surface.

And it was heading straight for him.

Ben froze as the shape rose slowly out of

the water. The fog was so thick that he couldn't make out what it was but it was moving slowly towards him. This thing was alive, and as dark as shadows. At first Ben thought it was a dog, or perhaps a person, but there was no way it could be either. Ben held his breath, gazing slowly upwards. The thing loomed over him, peering through large eyes. Ben gasped and slapped his hand over his mouth.

"Can't be..." he whispered.

But it was.

It was the Gorblimey.

The monster was exactly as Ben had imagined him: a plump, hairy thing, just a little taller than Ben and covered from head to toe in sodden fur so black that it seemed to drink any light that touched it. Coiled horns framed round, curious eyes, which almost seemed to glow. The Gorblimey let out a

gentle chirping sound like a bird, and his
candle flame flickered a bright yellow.

"*H-how?*" was all Ben could mutter as he got to his feet.

The Gorblimey let out a cheerful purr. Ben held out his hand. As ink-black fur enveloped his fingers, Ben laid his palm upon the monster's round belly. It was as warm as an electric blanket, and Ben could feel two hearts beating slowly.

The Gorblimey was real.

"Where did you come from?" Ben uttered, not quite able to believe his own eyes.

The Gorblimey hooted, twice. Then he held out a furry finger and pressed it lightly upon Ben's forehead.

"Did ... did I imagine you?" Ben whispered.

The Gorblimey nodded and the flame above his head glowed a warm, happy orange.

Without thinking, Ben waved his hand over the flame. It was ice-cold. Ben gasped again and the Gorblimey let out a low, rumbling chuckle.

"Ben!" came a sudden cry from the fog. Then another voice.

"Ben, are you out here?"

"Mum! Dad!" said Ben as the Gorblimey hooted nervously. Ben took the monster's hairy hand. "It's OK, it's my mum and dad," he assured him. "They're not going to believe what's—"

"There you are!" Ben's dad cried, finally spotting Ben through the mist. "Benjy, come back inside and let's talk ab— AAARGH!"

As the Gorblimey emerged through a haze of fog, Ben's dad let out a scream that was so loud it scattered seagulls from nearby chimneys. The Gorblimey immediately panicked. His candle flame flashed a bright blue and he scooped up Ben in his arms.

Ben heard a strange, high-pitched whistle emanating from every inch of the monster. He sounded like he was about to pop. Then:

POOOOOOM!

The Gorblimey launched them high into the air as if he'd been fired out of a cannon. By the time Ben's mum had called his name, both he and the Gorblimey had disappeared into the clouds.

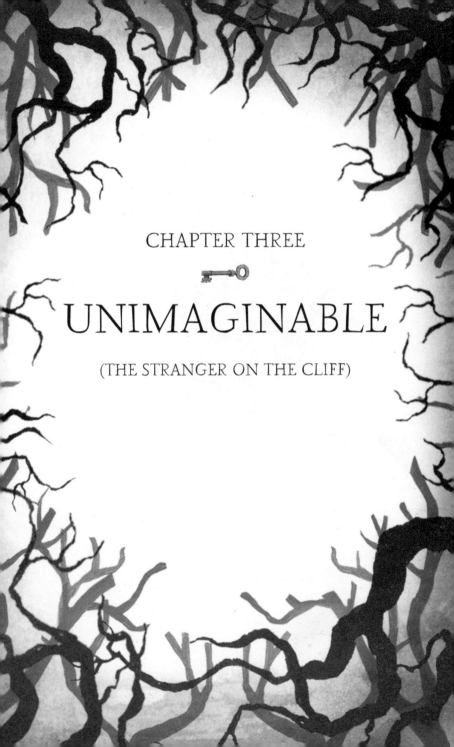

CHAPTER THREE

UNIMAGINABLE

(THE STRANGER ON THE CLIFF)

*"There is nothing more gladdening
than a trip to your imagining!"*
—SK

The Gorblimey soared high above the rooftops, with Ben held firmly in his arms. Ben screamed until his breath ran out.

As they arced through the sky, he saw the Gorblimey's candle flame still glowing blue with fear. A moment later, the monster began plummeting towards the ground. Ben saw the road rushing towards them. In seconds they would crash on to grey tarmac. "Oh no, no no!" he cried in horror. "GORBLI—"

POOOOM!

The Gorblimey bounced on the ground like a ball and launched back into the air as if he was made from rubber.

"AARGHahahaha!" Ben howled, so relieved that he wasn't dead that he screamed and laughed at the same time. The Gorblimey, too, let out a deep, echoing chuckle and his candle flame flickered a calm yellow. As the Gorblimey arced through the air and seagulls scattered in fear, Ben felt his face warmed by

a streak of sunlight breaking between grey-white clouds.

The pair of them bounced all over the island, past Mr Pinchpenny's You'll Be Lucky Casino, past the abandoned fairground with its long-deserted ghostly rides, past the burnt-out pier, past Grundy Island Zoo with its one sad giraffe ... even as far as the crazy golf course where Ben's dad worked.

After a little more bouncing, Ben and the Gorblimey settled on the edge of a high chalk cliff. They sat on soft, dewy grass and stared out over the ocean. It was late afternoon and the sun, hazy and half hidden behind cloud, had begun its slow descent to the horizon.

"My dad says you should never let your imagination run away with you," said Ben, peering out over the waves. "But I'm glad I imagined you."

The Gorblimey chirruped loudly. Then it let out a series of ringing cheeps, which Ben somehow understood perfectly.

"'Friends'? You mean, us?" Ben asked. Despite having imagined the Gorblimey in the first place, he was still surprised to hear the monster call him his friend. The Gorblimey nodded and let out a loud toot. "Yes! Of course! We're *best* friends. Best friends forever," Ben agreed. He felt a tear welling from the corner of his eye and quickly wiped it away. The Gorblimey tweeted happily and put a hairy arm round Ben's shoulder.

As the pair of them stared out to sea, it is not an overstatement to say that Ben Bunsen felt happier than ever before.

"I wonder how you went from being in here," Ben said at last, tapping the side of his head with his finger, "to being out here. What do you even call that?"

"*Unimaginary*," said a voice. Ben and the Gorblimey turned. Further along the cliff edge stood a lone figure, looking out over the ocean. He was tall, impossibly lean and dressed in a tailored suit with a long blue tailcoat and breeches, and buckled shoes over white stockings. The stranger wore a three-peaked hat that cast such a dark shadow over his face that Ben could barely make it out.

"Wh … what?" said Ben.

"That is what you call it when an imaginary friend travels from 'in here to out here' said the stranger, mimicking Ben's head-tapping. "When is an IF not an IF? When it is not simply imagined … it is unimagined. When it becomes *unimaginary*."

"Unimaginary…?" Ben repeated. He glanced at the Gorblimey, a shiver running down his spine.

"Truth is, some folk have *wild* imaginations," the stranger continued, still gazing out to sea. His voice clattered like pebbles shaken in a bucket. "The wilder the imagination, the wilder the unimaginary…"

Ben edged towards the stranger, craning to see the face hidden beneath the hat.

"How … how do you know that?" he asked.

The stranger laughed, his cackle dry as old sticks, and spun towards Ben.

"Oh, the things I know would curl your toes," he replied, lifting his hat off his head.

Ben stared into the face of a skull. Milk-white eyeballs floated in the skull's eye sockets and seemed to stare into Ben's soul.

"My name is Keys ... Skeleton Keys," it said. "And I have come for *you*."

CHAPTER FOUR

BEN'S UNIMAGINARY FRIEND

(AHOY, CAPTAIN GORBLIMEY!)

"A locked door is just a tale yet to be told."
—SK

Ben's second terrified scream of the day echoed across Grundy Island. Before the skeleton could act, a panicking Gorblimey leaped skywards again, grabbing Ben and bouncing away in an instant.

"I will find you, Benjamin Bunsen!" the skeleton cried as it watched Ben and the Gorblimey disappear into the clouds. Ben heard his name echo through the air.

The skeleton knew his name.

"Take us home, Gorblimey!" Ben cried. The monster duly obliged, returning Ben to his house in three great bounces. They had barely landed when Ben's mum and dad raced out of the front door.

"Ben! Are you all right?" cried Ben's dad as the Gorblimey placed Ben gently on the ground.

"W-what is that?" Ben's mum asked. The Gorblimey chirped nervously but Ben put his hand on the monster's arm and smiled.

"This is the Gorblimey," he said. "And he's my best friend."

Five minutes later, everyone was sitting round the table in the front room. An old radio played the local shipping forecast to no one in particular, and a log fire crackled away in the corner. In the middle of the table stood a large, near-complete replica of a pirate ship, built entirely from matches by Ben's dad. The ship took up nearly the whole table, as it had in their previous house, and the house before that. Usually, they would crane to look over it during dinner but today Ben's mum and dad peered over matchstick masts at a *monster*.

The Gorblimey tooted happily as he tucked into his fourth slice of birthday cake.

"How long's this been going on then?" Ben's mother said, staring at Ben's unimaginary friend in disbelief.

"How long's what been going on?" Ben asked.

"Don't play daft, Benjamin," his mum said. "Has the Gorblimey *always* been real? Where have you been keeping him all this time?"

"He's just been in my head 'til now," replied Ben.

"Well, we can't very well send him back there," sighed Ben's mum. "We'll have to do a shop. What does he eat?"

"He likes cake." Ben grinned as the Gorblimey shoved another slice into his mouth. The Gorblimey chirped in agreement and nodded so fast that his candle flame went out. He let out a panicked peep, and stuck his fingers in his ears. The next moment his cheeks puffed out and the flame flickered back into life.

"This'll take some getting used to," said Ben's mum with a smile.

"Now hang on, this is not the sort of thing you get 'used to'," said Ben's dad. He'd looked pale and sweaty-browed since he first laid eyes upon the Gorblimey. "An imaginary friend is supposed to be just that – *imaginary*. Do you remember that awful girl you made up when you were six? Debbie, was it?"

"Daisy," Ben corrected him.

"You blamed her for all sorts of terrible behaviour," Ben's dad continued. "It was a blessed relief when you finally forgot about her—"

"I *didn't* forget her," Ben interrupted. "We moved house again and Daisy didn't want to come with us."

"My point is your 'friends' are trouble enough when they're just in your head ... but *real*?" said Ben's dad. "I mean, what if this thing is dangerous?"

"Bob! What a thing to say!" said Ben's mum as the Gorblimey honked in dismay. "Ben imagined him – doesn't that make him our responsibility?"

"I'm just trying to be sensible about this," insisted Ben's dad. "Don't you think it'd be better off in a zoo than—"

"A *zoo*? The Gorblimey's not an animal!" Ben snapped. The Gorblimey let out a piercing squeal and panicked for the third time that day. Ben turned to see his friend vanish before his eyes. "Gorblimey! Where are you?"

The faintest whistling sound filled the room. Ben looked down at the table. There, standing on the deck of the matchstick pirate ship, was the Gorblimey, his candle flame a bright blue. He was no bigger than a chocolate bar.

"No *way*," said Ben, peering down at his tiny unimaginary friend. "You can shrink. You can really shrink!"

"Well, would you look at that, Bob – he's in perfect scale with your ship," said Ben's mum with a smile. "Ahoy there, Gorblimey!"

The Gorblimey made a sound like a ship's whistle. His flame flickered orange-yellow and he saluted, before proudly pacing up and down the deck.

"He … likes it?" said Ben's dad as the Gorblimey chirped happily. "He likes my ship?"

"And every ship needs a captain, doesn't it?" said Ben's mum, picking up the cake slice. "That settles it then – the Gorblimey is staying. Now, who wants another slice of—"

KNOCK.

KNOCK.

KNOCK.

There were three unnerving raps at the front door, then silence fell across the room.

"Who's that now?" Ben's mum said at last. She headed for the door. "Probably one of the neighbours wondering what on earth's going— Oh!"

Ben's mum stumbled backwards as the door swung open. There, standing in the doorway, was a tall, lean figure dressed in a long tailcoat and breeches and a three-peaked hat. His head lolled back to reveal his grinning skull of a face.

It was the skeleton.

CHAPTER FIVE

A SKELETON
AT THE DOOR

(KEY TO OBLIVION)

Whatever world you're living in,
'Tis better than Oblivion.
A place to visit? Better not!
One step inside and you're forgot!

"AAAAAAAAAAAAAAAAAAAAAAAAAAAAHHHHHHHHHHHHHHHHHHHHHHHH!"

No sooner had Ben's dad spotted the skeleton at the door than he let out a scream so loud and shrill that next door's skittish Schnauzer, Sullivan, started howling its head off.

"Ah, yes, I am quite a sight," the skeleton noted, a deathly smile fixed on his face. "I apologize if my appearance unsettles but skinless is how I came into this world, and skinless is how I remain."

Ben found himself holding his breath as he glanced back at the matchstick ship to see the shrunken Gorblimey duck behind a set of matchstick stairs leading to a matchstick poop deck.

"My grandmother taught me not to judge a book by its cover but I'm not sure I can take any more surprises today," said Ben's mum, tightening her grip on the cake slice in her hand. "Now, who are you, and what do you want?"

"My name is Keys ... Skeleton Keys," said the skeleton, taking off his hat and bowing deeply with a rattle of bones. "And I have come here for your son! Crumcrinkles, I only now hear how sinister that sounds..."

"You leave Ben alone!" roared Ben's dad. He grabbed the cake slice from Ben's mum and brandished it like a weapon. Before anyone knew what was happening, he was racing towards the skeleton.

"Dogs 'n' cats! I am in no mood for *rumbleshoving...*" declared Skeleton Keys. He bent down on one knee and sunk his right index finger, impossibly, into the floor. His finger turned with a CLICK-CLUNK and, in an instant, a trapdoor materialized in the floor.

"Bob, wait!" cried Ben's mum, leaping to stop Ben's dad, but as the pair collided the trapdoor swung open beneath their feet. They tumbled through it and vanished into darkness.

"Mum? Dad!" shrieked Ben. "What did you do with them?" he demanded as the skeleton slammed the trapdoor shut.

"Why, I transported them that-a-way, to the other end of your street!" replied Skeleton Keys. He waggled his forefinger. "I call this one the Key to a Quick Getaway ... it opens doors where there are none. A handy little trick, pun intentional, that has saved me from many an unimaginable fate." The skeleton glanced at his bony wrist as if looking at a watch. "I would say we have about two minutes to deal with your unimaginary problem..."

"P-problem?" Ben asked nervously, glancing

over to the matchstick ship to make sure the Gorblimey was well and truly hidden.

"Fret not! Ol' Mr Keys is a dab hand at dealing with unimaginaries," Skeleton Keys declared, the words rattling out of his mouth. "Once upon a previous life, I too existed in the mind of a child ... until the day her imaginings became so wild that I was suddenly as real as bad breath."

"*You're* an imaginary friend?" asked Ben.

"I was ... though it has been an age since anyone called me 'friend'," replied Skeleton Keys with a sigh. He made his way to the fireplace and placed his hat on the mantelpiece. "These days I have a lonelier purpose – keeping a watchful eye socket on the recently unimagined! So, there I was, besnoozed at home in my *Doorminion*, when lo and behold, I got *the twitch*. It is always a confuddling feeling, the twitch – a most peculiar rattle of the bones! But it can mean only one thing – an IF has become unimaginary." Skeleton Keys gazed into the fire and rubbed his eye sockets with his fingers. "But I only get this awful skull-ache if the unimaginary is *dangerous*."

"Dangerous?" repeated Ben. "But the Gorblimey isn't—"

"An IF is all very well when they exist in your mind but when they become unimaginary, that is a whole other bag o' hamsters!" interrupted Skeleton Keys. He picked up an iron poker from the fireplace and jabbed at the burning logs. "If an unimaginary proves too dangerous for the real world, it is up to me to prevent chaos and calamity, not to mention catastrophe. So, where is he? Where is the beast that abducted you?"

"I ... I don't understand," Ben muttered, doing everything he could not to look at the pirate ship.

"He must be close by – the twitch led me to your door," explained Skeleton Keys. He swung round, waggling the little finger on his right hand. "Fret not! Ol' Mr Keys can end his wild ways, for I have this!"

"A finger?" Ben asked nervously.

"No, *this*," tutted the skeleton, pointing to his fingertip. Like the rest, it was shaped like a key. "For these fantabulant fingers o' mine can open doors to hidden worlds and secret places," he added. "And *this* one is *the Key to Oblivion*."

"What's Oblivion?" asked Ben as the Gorblimey stifled a fearful chirrup.

"A prison of nothingness!" declared Skeleton Keys. "To be banished to the endless void of Oblivion is to disappear, to vanish

... even from the faintest memory! Those who find themselves there are doomed to be *forgotten*. I am not going to lie, it is absolutely rubbish."

The Gorblimey couldn't stop himself letting out the tiniest terrified toot. The skeleton spun on his heels towards the matchstick ship and loomed over it, his sunken sockets scanning every inch of the miniature deck. The tiny Gorblimey froze but it was too late – he'd been spotted. Skeleton Keys unfurled his long, key-like fingers, brandishing them like weapons.

"Ah," he said. "*There* you are."

CHAPTER SIX

DANGEROUS

(SOME THINGS ARE BEST FORGOTTEN)

TOP 5 UNIMAGINARIES OF NOTE:
The Loch Ness Monster
Bigfoot
Count Dracula
Queen Victoria
Albert Einstein

"Ignoble creation of a child's overactive imagination!" cried Skeleton Keys, rounding on the tiny Gorblimey as he backed away across the matchstick deck. "No more will you plague this poor stripling!"

"But the Gorblimey's not—" was all Ben managed to get out before the terrified Gorblimey let out his high-pitched whistle. With a tiny POOOOOOM! the minuscule monster leaped into the air and ricocheted off the ceiling, before bouncing around the room like a pinball.

"Dogs 'n' cats! He has a trick or two up his nose, this one!" shrieked Skeleton Keys, desperately trying to grab the Gorblimey as it whizzed around with a POOOOOOM! POOOOOOM! POOOOOOM!, shattering ornaments and light bulbs. "He is slipperier than sardines on a soap dish!" declared Skeleton Keys. "But I can be tricky too!"

As the Gorblimey rebounded off one wall and headed for another, Skeleton Keys thrust the *Key to a Quick Getaway* into the wall and turned it with a *CLICK-CLUNK*. A doorway materialized in the wall and the skeleton swung it open. The Gorblimey was moving too fast to stop – he shot through the doorway and disappeared.

"Gorblimey!" Ben shouted. A split second later, the transported Gorblimey reappeared through the kitchen doorway. Skeleton Keys was waiting for him – he stretched out a long arm and grabbed the flying Gorblimey as he zoomed past.

"Gotcha!" cried Skeleton Keys, his little finger poised and ready. "Your reign of terror is over – Oblivion awaits!"

"Wait!" Ben cried, the Gorblimey hooting in horror. "The Gorblimey isn't dangerous! He's my friend!"

"Yes, he *is* a fiend!" the skeleton said. "Brute, release the child from your— Wait, did you say 'friend'?"

"Yes! The Gorblimey is my *best* friend!" cried Ben. Skeleton Keys froze, the Gorblimey still struggling in his grip.

"Best ... friend?" repeated Skeleton Keys. He suddenly lunged towards Ben, so close that Ben flinched backwards. "Are you sure? Blink twice and make the sound of a peacock if he is holding you against your will..."

"What? No, he's not!" cried Ben.

"But the twitch is never wrong! Except that one time ... twice if you count the incident with the unicorn," mused Skeleton Keys.

"Well, the Gorblimey is *not* dangerous – he's not!" Ben said as firmly as he could. A dubious Skeleton Keys placed the monster carefully on the kitchen table and peered at it, his head cocked suspiciously to one side.

"Miscreant monster, you clearly have this child spellbound," Skeleton Keys cried, rolling his head from one side to the other. "The unimaginary must be a threat! A wild imagination runs in the family, and after what happened with your father..."

"My dad?" Ben said as the skeleton trailed off. "What do you mean? What happened with my dad?"

Skeleton Keys paused, and though his skull was fixed in a grim, expressionless visage, Ben was sure he saw a sudden look of sadness on the skeleton's face.

"That is a confuddling tale ... and some things are best forgotten," Skeleton Keys sighed. He peered wistfully at the pirate ship made from matchsticks, and added, "Though he still dreams of the sea, I see..."

"I don't understand," Ben said. Then suddenly came the panicked cries of his mum and dad as they raced down the street towards the house.

"I am afraid we are out of time, for the time being," said Skeleton Keys. He loped over to a nearby chest of drawers and opened one of the drawers to find it filled with hundreds of matchboxes. He closed the drawer, slipped another key-shaped finger into its lock and turned with a *CLICK-CLUNK*.

When he opened the drawer again, Ben noticed it was empty and as black as a night full of shadows. Skeleton Keys quickly clambered inside. "I shall take my leave for now ... but I will be keeping my eye sockets on you, monster," he said, eyeing the

Gorblimey. "Should you be tempted to show your true colours, remember I am only ever a door away..."

"Ben!"

As Ben's mum and dad burst through the front door, Skeleton Keys disappeared inside the drawer as if it were as deep as a well. It slammed shut, seemingly of its own accord. By the time Ben's dad had wrenched it back open, Skeleton Keys was gone and the drawer was full of matchboxes once more.

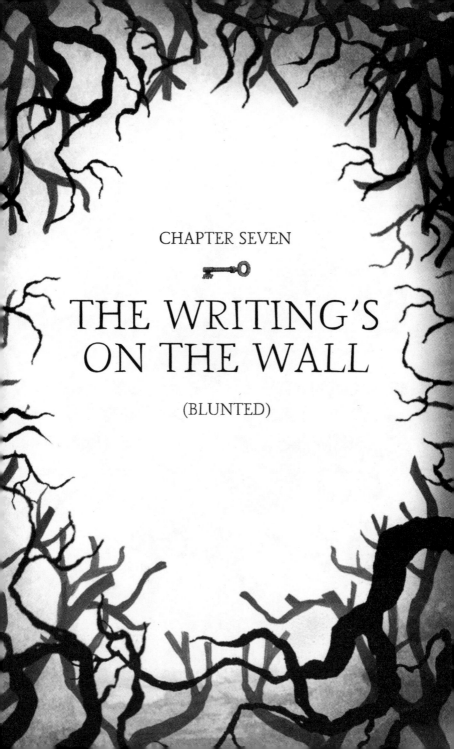

CHAPTER SEVEN

THE WRITING'S ON THE WALL

(BLUNTED)

*"I have the key.
I have the secret."*
—SK

Ben's dad upturned the drawer, spilling matchboxes all over the floor. Skeleton Keys had disappeared and the drawer was no longer a mysterious escape route. The drawer was just a drawer.

"Ben!" cried Ben's mum, rushing over to him. "Are you all right?"

"Mum, I'm fiiiiine," Ben protested, not enjoying being fussed over in front of his best friend – but loving the fact that he had a best friend to be embarrassed in front of.

"What *was* that thing?" asked Ben's dad,

frantically pulling out the other drawers and scattering matches all over the floor. "What did he want? Did he say anything to you, Ben?"

Ben collected the shrunken Gorblimey from the table. As he cradled his best friend in his palm, Ben decided there was no way he was telling his dad the real reason for Skeleton Keys' visit. Instead he said, "He, uh, didn't say anything much. But he *knew* who you were, Dad."

"Me?" said Ben's dad, taken aback. "I think I'd remember meeting a living skeleton!"

"You certainly went a funny colour when you saw him," said Ben's mum. "And you did an *awful* lot of screaming..."

"He was a skeleton! Excuse me for being spooked! What was I supposed to do, ask him in for a cup of tea?" Ben's dad glowered at his son. "Ben, I want you to promise me that if you ever meet the skeleton man again, you'll run as fast as you can, do you understand?"

"But—" Ben began.

"Promise me!" snapped Ben's dad. "Promise me, or it's the zoo for your monster!"

"Bob! Take that back!" Ben's mum cried, but Ben was already picturing the Gorblimey locked in a cage in Grundy Island Zoo, afraid and alone but for the company of the zoo's one sad giraffe.

"I—" began Ben's dad, but Ben let out a grunt, half nervous and half defiant, and backed away. Then, with the shrunken Gorblimey still cupped in his palm, he raced upstairs. He could already hear his parents arguing as he climbed the ladder to his bedroom.

"Dad treats me like a *kid*," Ben complained, placing the Gorblimey on his bed. The monster grew to normal size in an instant and let out a low gargling sound. "I know, but Dad treats me like a *little* kid – like I'm nine," Ben replied. "He's just jealous 'cause he hasn't got any friends except Mum and she doesn't count 'cause they're married. He'd rather spend all day with that stupid matchstick boat..."

The Gorblimey emitted a goose-like honk and gave Ben a huge, hairy hug. Ben got hair up his nose and laughed as he tried to stifle a sneeze.

"You're welcome!" he said. "I can't believe Skeleton Keys thought you were dangerous. How could he—"

The Gorblimey suddenly let Ben go and stepped back. He stared past Ben, his candle flame flickering blue once more.

"Gorblimey? What is it?" Ben asked. The Gorblimey raised a hairy hand and pointed at the wall. Ben turned. Scrawled in pencil crayon and covering the entire wall were the words...

You forgot about ME

Ben's blood ran cold.

"What...?" he muttered. He turned to the Gorblimey. "Did ... you write that?"

The Gorblimey trumpeted like a hippo, a little offended by the suggestion, and then let out a shrill tweet.

"Of course not – why would I write on my own wall?" Ben looked down at the floor. He picked up a pencil crayon and saw it was blunted. In fact, the floor was strewn with blunted pencils. Someone had flattened them all to nubs delivering their message.

But who?

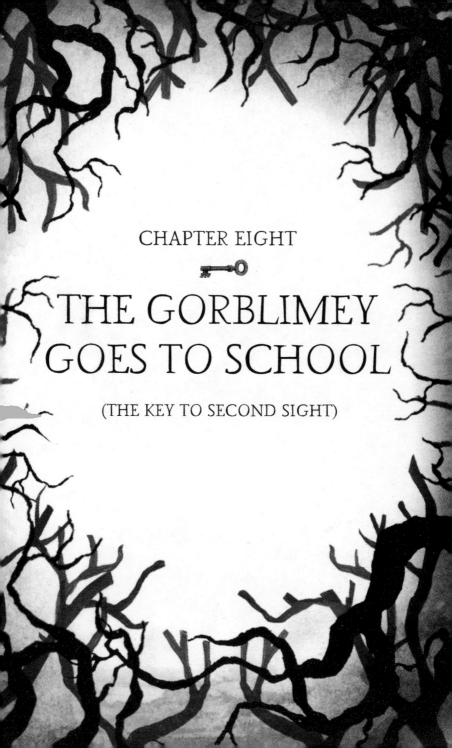

CHAPTER EIGHT

THE GORBLIMEY GOES TO SCHOOL

(THE KEY TO SECOND SIGHT)

See what you can't? You may, you might
Just turn the Key to Second Sight!

"'You forgot about me'," Ben whispered, staring at the words on his wall. One way or another, he was sure the Gorblimey would get the blame. Before his mum came to check on him, Ben found a rolled-up poster under his bed that his dad had given him (for an old film entitled *The Pirates of Octopus Island*) and he and the Gorblimey stuck it up over the words on the wall.

But it didn't change the fact that someone had written them.

Ben hadn't slept a wink by the time the seagulls began their morning racket. The Gorblimey had spent the night curled up asleep on top of Ben's wardrobe but it wasn't the monster's loud snoring that kept him awake – Ben's mind raced with questions. Everything had taken a turn for the strange since he'd unimagined the Gorblimey but there was one thing Ben was sure of: he wasn't about to give up the first real friend he'd ever had.

"You need to be at school in thirty minutes, Ben Bunsen," said Ben's mum, poking her head up through the attic door. "How's the new addition to the family?"

"He snores," replied Ben with a yawn. "A lot."

"Well then, there's something he has in common with your dad," replied Ben's mum with a wink. Ben rubbed his eyes.

"Mum, the Gorblimey isn't dangerous," he whispered. "I promise."

"If I thought he was, he wouldn't be staying under my roof," said his mum. "And don't worry about your dad, he's just ... cautious. Your grandma used to say he was never the same after their house fell down when he was a boy. They never did find out how it happened..." Ben's mum looked lost in thought for a moment, before putting on her serious face. "Right, you – dressed and out of the house in twenty minutes. I'm at the surgery 'til five and your dad's closing up the crazy golf, so don't forget your front door key. Help yourself to a snack when you get in. No more cake."

"OK," said Ben as his mum disappeared back down the ladder. He looked up at the snoring Gorblimey. There was no way he was leaving him in the house. What if Skeleton

Keys came back to send him to Oblivion?
Then again, he couldn't very well take the
Gorblimey to school.

Could he?

"Seeyoulaterbye!" Ben blurted as he rushed
downstairs. Ben's mum and dad barely had
time to look up from the breakfast table
before the door slammed shut.

"Are you all right in there?" said Ben as he
hurried down the cobbled street through a
haze of drizzle to school. He opened his jacket
and peeked inside. There was the Gorblimey,
shrunken and nestled in his pocket, looking
altogether uneasy and emitting trembling
toots. "Don't worry, it'll be OK," Ben assured
him. "No one will ever know…"

"No one will ever know what?" said a voice.
Ben turned to see a skeleton in a tailored suit

and three-peaked hat walking briskly alongside him. Ben shrieked loudly and pulled his jacket tightly around him. "Actually, would you mind *not* howling with fright?" Skeleton Keys asked. "I would rather not draw attention to myself – and I am a tad too skeletal to pass for a passer-by," he added, pulling his hat low. "Now, where is the unimaginary? This twitch o' mine is giving my skull a gut ache. I am still as determined as I am dapper that the beast is dangerous..."

"The Gorblimey's not done anything," said Ben, nervously zipping up his jacket. "I ... I haven't even seen him this morning..."

"Gone into hiding, eh? No doubt planning something fiendishly foul," exclaimed Skeleton Keys. "On a scale of one to off-the-scale, how mischievous, spiteful, hurtful, barbarous, vile, wicked, or wickedly vile has the unimaginary been towards you or your—?"

"He's none of those! He's my friend!" Ben interrupted. He spied the school. Beyond the gates, he could see children milling about, waiting for the morning bell.

Ben picked up the pace.

"Don't be foolboozled, Benjamin, my twitch is never wrong – the monster will make his move soon enough," said Skeleton Keys, keeping up with long strides of his bone legs. "And when he does, whoosh! Off to Oblivion! Perhaps not with a 'whoosh' ... maybe a 'swoof' or a 'swiiish' or a— School!" Skeleton Keys all but skidded to a halt as he spotted the gates. "Why, I have not been to one of these in an age! Schools are a positive haven for IFs!"

"I should go in," said Ben, desperate to get away.

"Cheese 'n' biscuits! There are imaginings everywhere, look!" declared Skeleton Keys.

"But of course, you cannot! Here, let me fix that…"

The skeleton held up the third finger on his left hand and pointed it between Ben's eyes. He turned it, and Ben heard the *CLICK-CLUNK* of a key turning in a lock – but not in his ears … in his *mind*. Ben felt his actual thoughts shiver and shake.

"What was that…?" Ben asked, his eyes wide and wild.

"I call it *the Key to Second Sight*," Skeleton Keys replied. "It allows you to gaze, if only for a few moments, beyond the real to the imagined. Here, take a gaddly good gander at your classfellows…"

Ben peered again at the children gathering for the school day. They were all there – Cliff Pitchfork, Hattie Blanket, Ichabod Twist and the rest – everyone Ben's mum and dad had invited to his party … everyone Ben hoped might be his friend, if only they had a reason to notice him. But then Ben spotted something.

Hattie Blanket had a full-grown crocodile walking by her side.

A crocodile!

"What...?" Ben muttered. The next

moment, he saw Cliff Pitchfork wandering around the playground flanked by a boy and a girl. They held up placards that read *I AM BOY* and *I AM GIRL*. It took Ben a moment to notice that neither of them had faces.

Ichabod Twist's companion was a dog at one end and a cat at the other. The dog end of the creature wore a large, conical anti-scratch collar around its neck, while the cat end meowed judgmentally at its other half.

"What ... what are they?" asked Ben. He felt the Gorblimey fidget in his pocket.

"They are IFs – your classfellows' imaginary friends," replied Skeleton Keys. "I am sure you have considered yourself quite different, Benjamin – but believe you me, everyone is different in their own way. Difference is what makes life gladdening. Perhaps your imaginings are a tad wilder than others' ... but a wild imagination can change the world."

"I never knew..." Ben said, gazing wide-eyed at the myriad imaginary friends accompanying his classmates.

"Of course, *your* wild imagination has

almost certainly unleashed a foulsome beast upon the world," clarified Skeleton Keys, examining *the Key to Oblivion* at the end of his finger. "But do not worry, Ol' Mr Keys is on the case! You can rely on me to— Benjamin?"

Skeleton Keys looked round to see Ben racing through the gates and into school.

"Nice to see a child who appreciates the value of education," said Skeleton Keys. "Now, where *is* that unimaginary..."

CHAPTER NINE

THE BIG REVEAL

(UNVEILING THE GORBLIMEY)

UNIMAGINARIES MOST OFT
MISTAKEN FOR SOMETHING ELSE
Aliens
Werewolves
Zombies
Teachers

B en sat through registration, gazing in awe at his classmates' imaginary friends. The IFs came and went like ghosts, whenever the children imagined them. *If only they knew,* Ben thought as the shrunken Gorblimey squirmed in his jacket.

By the time the effects of his second sight had started to fade (and his classmates' IFs with it), Ben had fixed upon an idea that he was sure would change everything: he was going to introduce everyone to the Gorblimey. Since Ben's classmates had IFs too, they would surely climb over each other to get to know Ben and his *unimaginary* friend. Ben would have more friends than he knew what to do with! And once everyone was friends, Skeleton Keys would realize his mistake and leave them well alone.

Ben followed the rest of his class to the hall for assembly. He gazed around at the children sitting in silent rows. The whole school was there – it was the perfect place for his *big reveal*.

"When I say '*now*', you bounce out and grow," Ben whispered into his pocket as he followed the other children into the hall. The tiny monster fidgeted anxiously. "Don't worry, you'll be *great*," Ben reassured him. "Just try not to tread on anyone when you jump out..."

Ben waited for two agonizing minutes as the head teacher, Ms Mercy, droned on about punctuality. The second she paused for breath, Ben seized his moment. He stood up and nervously cleared his throat. The whole school turned and stared.

"I ... I have something to show you," he said. He held open the right side of his jacket and whispered, "OK ... *now.*"

There was a pause.

A long pause.

"Go ... I mean, *grow*," whispered Ben, giving his jacket a shake.

Another pause, even longer.

Someone at the back of the hall coughed.

"Gorblimey...?" Ben muttered, peering inside the pocket. There, illuminated by a tiny blue candle flame, was the monster, shaking his head and trying to retreat further into Ben's pocket. "It's OK!" Ben whispered. "You can do it..."

"Benjamin...?" said Ms Mercy.

"*Please*, Gorblimey…" whispered Ben, but by now the Gorlimey was so small that Ben could barely make out the faint glow of his candle flame.

"Weirdo," said Cliff Pitchfork behind him.

A peel of sniggers rang out across the hall. Ben felt his face turning hot, beetroot-red.

"Do you have something to say, Benjamin?" Ms Mercy asked.

"I...I..." he muttered, letting go of his jacket. Whispers of "weirdo" echoed around the hall, and the sniggering grew louder as Ben stood there, turning redder by the second, and shook his head.

"Then go and wait outside my office, please," said Ms Mercy impatiently.

The whole hall stared as Ben made his way awkwardly through the sea of children. All he could think about was how Skeleton Keys had described Oblivion – a prison of nothingness,

where you're doomed to be forgotten. In
that moment, Ben wished he himself could
disappear ... vanish ... even from the faintest
memory.

Ten minutes later, Ben was in the middle
of a long corridor, sitting on the popularly
nicknamed Chair of Doom outside the head
teacher's office. Hattie Blanket came out of
the girls' toilet opposite.

"Weirdo," she mouthed, shooting him a
withering look as she passed. As far as Ben
knew, it was the first time she'd ever noticed
him, but he'd really rather she hadn't. He
sighed and waited until she was out of
earshot.

"Gorblimey...?" Ben whispered, opening his
jacket. He heard a long, apologetic coo and
saw the shrunken Gorblimey's head poking

out of his pocket. "No, *I'm* sorry," Ben said. "I shouldn't have pushed you into it. I know how scared you get. I just thought if everyone met you then..."

Ben trailed off as the lights in the corridor flickered. He glanced to his left. At the end of the long corridor, he saw a lone figure standing as still as a statue. It was a girl. She was even shorter than Ben, with pigtails and a striped dress and polished shoes over wrinkled socks. Her skin, hair and clothing were grey, as if she had stepped out of a black and white photograph.

And her head was on backwards.

Ben's jaw fell open.

"Can't be..." he blurted. "*Daisy?*"

P ardon the interruption, dallywanglers! I do hope you are enjoying the tale of Ben's unimaginary friend. I do not know about you but I find the character of the heroic, key-fingered skeleton *especially* compelling...

Anyway, we are about halfway through Ben's uncanny adventure, and things are about to take a turn for the twisted, so I thought now might be a good time to make yourself a nice cup of tea and pop to the loo for necessary doings. I shall wait...

...Ah, you are back – *fabulush*! I hope everything went according to plan. Now then, where were we? If I remember rightly, which a storyteller always must, Ben had just had an important revelation and with it, he spoke a single word – *Daisy*.

As you have already learned, the Gorblimey

was not Ben Bunsen's first imaginary friend. His first IF went by the name of Daisy. Ben first imagined the girl with the backwards head on his sixth birthday. He was swinging a shiny, spanking-new toy sword around his bedroom and imagining himself to be quite the swashbuckler. The plastic cutlass swung this-a-way and that, that-a-way and this... Suddenly, Ben's mother and father heard the most ear-worrying echo around the house. They rushed upstairs to find Ben, sword in hand, standing over a shattered bedside lamp lying on the floor.

Ben was quick to insist that *Daisy* was to blame. Naturally, Ben's father asked who "Daisy" was, and Ben explained that she was a girl with a backwards head ... a girl who could turn invisible ... a girl who liked to *break* things. Ben's parents quickly realized what had happened – Ben had imagined his first IF.

Ben blamed *all* of his bad behaviour upon Daisy. He claimed she was a rude-brained rumbleshover who took pleasure in making mess and mischief. Breakages occurred on an almost daily basis. "Don't tell me, Daisy did it," Ben's mother and father would sigh. Behind closed doors, they even started to call him "Bad Ben"...

But oddly enough, Daisy was not even kind to Ben, despite being a figment of his imaginings. Ben would claim she had torn up his drawings or hidden his asthma inhaler or tripped him over. Once, she set fire to all of his shoes. In the end, even Ben was not sure he wanted Daisy around, but she was in his head and not going anywhere.

That is, until the Bunsens moved house. Ben was seven years old when his father insisted on relocating the family yet again. Ben's father also suggested it was a chance for

Ben to put his bad behaviour behind him –
and perhaps even make some real friends.

Ben decided that his imaginary friend did
not *want* to leave. So, when the Bunsens
packed a removals van and drove away, Daisy
stayed behind. In the weeks and months that
followed, Ben thought of his friend often but
he did not *imagine* her in the way he once
had. He had to admit, it was a relief not to be
constantly getting into trouble all the time. In
time, Ben imagined a new IF, the Gorblimey,
who was kind, gentle and just a little nervous,
and Ben turned over a new leaf – although he
was no better at making real friends.

So then! Since you are now an expert on the
girl with the backwards head, let us reunite
with Ben Bunsen where we left him, all those
words ago. Can it really be that he has just
seen Daisy in the school corridor, as plain
as crisps? Ben's mind is racing faster than a

dog chasing another dog chasing a cat. He has not the faintest idea what might happen next. For, as I think I might have mentioned, strange things can happen when imaginations run wild...

CHAPTER TEN

THE RETURN OF DAISY

(RIGGED)

*"'Tis like a scratch I cannot itch,
but I can always trust the twitch!"*
—SK

Ben stared, unblinking, at the girl with the backwards head. The lights in the corridor suddenly flickered again.

Daisy was gone.

Vanished, as if she was never there.

Ben rubbed his eyes. It couldn't have been Daisy! It had to be the effect of *the Key to Second Sight* – a strange echo of his own imagination making him see things. Without thinking, Ben found himself walking down the now empty corridor. He spotted something on the floor where Daisy had been standing. Ben reached down and picked it up.

It was a box of matches – the same brand that his dad used to build his ship. Ben inspected the box. On the back were three words written in pencil crayon:

You forgot ME

Ben gasped. The Gorblimey let out a confused chirp from inside his jacket pocket.

"It's really her ... she's really *real*," he muttered, staring at the matchbox.

"Gorblimey, it's Daisy! She's here. She's unimaginary!" The Gorblimey let out a series of jittery squeaks, like a baby crocodile.

"I know, that's why I'm worried. Daisy is danger—"

Before the word fully escaped his lips, a terrifying possibility struck Ben so hard it took his breath away. What if Skeleton Keys was right? His uncanny twitch was convinced that Ben's unimaginary friend was *dangerous* – but what if he was after the *wrong* unimaginary friend?

"I didn't unimagine her ... did I?" Ben muttered with a shiver of dread. He hadn't thought about Daisy in years – how could she be here? How could she be real?

Ben inspected the matchbox.

"She must have been home," he said. "We have to find her. She's bound to be planning someth—"

"Benjamin Bunsen," said a voice. Ben spun round to see Ms Mercy looming over him, her arms folded. "I thought I told you to wait outside my office..."

Five minutes later, Ben was standing inside the head teacher's office. As Ms Mercy lectured him about the importance of respect, he stared at the matchbox in his hand. Daisy was planning something – something *terrible* – he just knew it. He had to get out of there and quickly. But how?

"The last person who interrupted me in an assembly disappeared without a trace," said Ms Mercy, tapping long fingernails on her desk. "Would you care to tell me what that little *display* was all ab—"

"I need to go!" blurted Ben. The head glowered at him in genuine shock. "I-I mean, please, miss, I've really got to go, it's important..."

"Despite what you might read on toilet walls, I am not a monster, Benjamin," said Ms Mercy. "But that's the *second* time you've interrupted me today. Give me one good reason why I should release you from my clutches?"

"I-I..." Ben began, but then he felt the Gorblimey move in his pocket. No, not move – *grow*. Before Ben knew what was happening, the Gorblimey had grown so large and so quickly that Ben's jacket had split open. The monster tumbled on to Ms Mercy's desk and stood up, rising to his full height. He loomed over the head teacher, glowering at her through piercing eyes, his candle flame glowing intensely. Ms Mercy shrunk back into her chair, her eyes wide with horror.

"Y-you're dismissed," she whimpered.

Thirty seconds later, Ben and the Gorblimey were flying through the air.

"Did you see Ms Mercy's face? That was – you were – great!" cried Ben as they soared over Grundy Island, propelled by the monster's bounces. The Gorblimey made a guttural, hippo-like grunt. "Of course I think you're brave!" Ben replied. Then he thought but did not say, *We'll both need to be brave if we find Daisy.*

In moments, Ben's house was in sight. The Gorblimey plummeted towards the ground and landed by the front door. Ben checked his watch – his mum and dad would be at work by now. He fumbled in his trouser pocket for his key, shoved it into the lock and pushed open the door.

The first things Ben noticed were the hundred or so matchboxes scattered all over the table and floor.

He looked up and spotted his dad's pirate ship on the table. It was surrounded by fireworks – the ones his parents had bought for his birthday party. There were dozens of brightly coloured tubes, piled up around the ship like waves crashing against its hull, or jammed in between the masts. The ship was rigged for destruction.

"Hello, crybaby," said a disembodied voice. A moment later Daisy appeared out of thin air in front of the table. While her body faced the mountain of fireworks, Daisy's backwards head peered straight at Ben. He saw that lopsided grin spread across her ashen face and realized she was holding a box of matches.

Daisy struck a match against the box. In an instant, the flame flickered into life.

"Daisy, what are you—?" Ben began. "Oh no."

"Oh yes," said Daisy, flicking the match into the fireworks mountain. "I'd run if I was you."

CHAPTER ELEVEN

FIREWORKS

(THE KEY TO POSSIBILITY)

With but the turn of a key,
it is possible to make the impossible, improbable,
inconceivable and unimaginable possible!
Possibly.

"Gorblimey, go! Run!" Ben screamed as he heard the hiss and fizz of the fireworks. As Daisy vanished, Ben turned on his heels. He shoved the Gorblimey out of the front door and on to the pavement.

BOOM.

Ben glanced back through the open door

BANG after

CRACK after

BOOOOOM after

FWEeEeEeEeE filled the air as the
fireworks exploded, emitting colourful sprays
of sparks. Ben and the Gorblimey watched
in horror as the fireworks continued to
WHiiiiZZ and FOOOSH
and KA-BANG!

In moments the room was ablaze.

"The twitch is never wrong..." said a
clattering voice. Ben glanced behind him to
see a pair of polished black shoes and thin,
stocking-clad legs. He peered up, and Skeleton
Keys glared down at him.

"It wasn't the Gorblimey!" Ben cried. "It
was—"

"I shall deal with the monster
momentarily!" interrupted Skeleton Keys,
striding past them towards the burning room.
"But first let us get this impromptu inferno
under control before it burns your house to
the—AAARGH!"

The last of the fireworks smashed through the front window. Skeleton Keys threw himself to the ground with a clatter of bones as the rocket exploded in mid-air, just above his head.

"Crumcrinkles, it has been a while since I have been struck in the bony bits by a whippadeedooo! Not an experience I care to repeat," Skeleton Keys said, crawling to the front door on all fours. He quickly pulled the door shut and dragged himself to his feet, brushing at the singed sleeve of his jacket. "This calls for *the Key to Possibility*! For anything is possible when *the Key to Possibility* makes anything possible – possibly." Skeleton Keys inserted the middle finger on his right hand into the door and turned it with a *CLICK-CLUNK*. "It never fails! Usually."

Skeleton Keys swung open the door. Ben

gasped. It was raining – *inside* the front room.
Water poured down in gallons from grey
clouds gathered on the ceiling, dousing the
flames in a matter of seconds.

"No *way*," Ben said, watching, open-
mouthed, as the rain fell in torrents.

"See? Never fails!" said a relieved Skeleton
Keys. As Ben edged towards the front door,
the rain stopped as quickly as it had started,
the clouds fading to nothing in an instant.
Ben stood in the doorway, the last of the
rainwater washing over his feet, then slowly
made his way inside. The room was charred
and scorched, and burn marks covered
the walls, ceiling and floor. The table was
upturned and blackened by fire, and the once
proud matchstick pirate ship that stood upon
it was no more. It had been blown to pieces,
and the pieces burned to ash.

Skeleton Keys and the Gorblimey followed

Ben inside. There was a long, strange silence, without so much as the squawk of a seagull outside. At last, Ben whispered:

"This is my fault."

"Flabberjabs! This unimaginary is to blame!" howled Skeleton Keys, rounding on the Gorblimey and pointing a key-tipped finger at him. "Ol' Mr Keys was right all along – he is too dangerous!"

"But the Gorblimey didn't do it!" said Ben as the monster emitted a thin, helpless whistle. "It was Daisy!"

"That is what they all say!" said Skeleton Keys. "Actually, no one has ever said that. Who or what is 'Daisy'?"

"My other imaginary friend! My *first* imaginary friend," Ben explained. "I saw her at school ... I *actually* saw her. She's real!"

"*Another* unimaginary? I have heard some tall stories but that is one you could climb," Skeleton Keys sneered, eyeballing the Gorblimey. "You may have spellbound the boy with your lies, beast, but I was not born yesterday. Technically, I was not born at all but that is beside the point. I will not fail this family again! It's Oblivion for you!"

"But you can't!" Ben cried as Skeleton Keys pulled the front door shut.

"But I *must*," the skeleton added, aiming his little finger at the lock. "And any door can be the door to Oblivion ... even this one."

"Don't!" Ben cried, grabbing Skeleton Keys' finger. He grappled with the skeleton, trying with all his might to stop him from turning the key. The Gorblimey hooted, taking a step towards Ben. "No!" Ben shouted. "Get out of here! Run!"

The Gorblimey shook his head, desperate to help and horrified at the thought of abandoning his friend.

"I mean it!" roared Ben as Skeleton Keys edged the *Key to Oblivion* towards the lock. "Run, Gorblimey! Run!"

The Gorblimey made a sound Ben had never heard before, like the desperate song of a lost whale. Ben howled one more desperate "RUN!" before his best friend's groans gave way to a high-pitched whistle. There was a crackle of electricity and a moment later, the Gorblimey launched himself out of the window with a

POOOM!

Ben watched his friend leap high into the grey sky and disappear into the clouds. All that was left was the echoing sound of his explosive bounce.

The Gorblimey was gone.

"Dogs 'n' cats, he got away!" huffed Skeleton Keys as Ben let go of his finger. "But fret not! Ol' Mr Keys will not rest until—"

"It wasn't him!" Ben yelled, tears streaming down his face. "I told you! I told you it was Daisy!"

"Benjamin, I have been dealing with the unimagined since before your great-grandparents had great-grandparents," explained Skeleton Keys. "I think I would know if there was another unimaginary on the loose. My twitch, lest we forget, is never—"

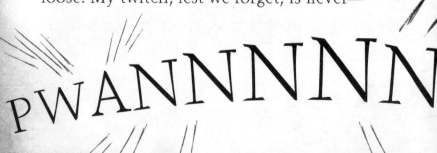

PWANNNN

Ben didn't see Daisy appear from inside the fireplace. He didn't notice the iron poker held tightly in her hands. He didn't even see it swinging through the air towards Skeleton Keys' head. What he did see was the skeleton's head fly from his neck and through the air. The head collided with Ben's chest before bouncing along the floor and skidding to a halt. Ben watched in silent horror as the headless Skeleton Keys slumped to the floor with a bony clatter.

"Goes on a bit, doesn't he?" said Daisy, flinging the poker to the floor with a *CLANG*.

"D-Daisy!" Ben cried, unable to take his eyes off Skeleton Keys' decapitated head. "What did you do?"

"That's nothing," she said, her lopsided grin spreading across her face. "Wait 'til you see what I do *next*."

CHAPTER TWELVE

THE GIRL
WITH THE
BACKWARDS
HEAD

(CRYBABY)

"I never feel at home
if I'm missing just one bone."
—SK

"Look what you did!" Ben howled, peering in horror at the disembodied skull lying at his feet. "Why would you do that?"

"I can't believe you're ten – you still whine like a six-year-old," Daisy tutted. "If I had a phone I'd report you to the crybaby police ... and then I'd smack you with it."

"But you killed him!" growled Ben. Daisy shrugged.

"He's a skeleton, isn't he dead already?"

"That's not the point!" Ben said angrily.

"How are you even here? I didn't imagine you
... did I?"

"You didn't *mean* to, maybe," Daisy replied.
"But even when you forgot me I must still
have been there, in some dark corner of your
mind. Otherwise how did I appear on that
beach yesterday?"

"Is that ... is that when I unimagined you?"
asked Ben. "I didn't see you..."

"I was *invisible*, you soggy bog roll," said
Daisy. "Not that you'd have noticed anyway –
you weren't trying to imagine me, were you?
You were trying to imagine *him*."

"Him?" Ben repeated, though he knew
exactly who she was talking about.

"Don't play dumb, dummy," huffed Daisy.
"Fluffy McCandlehead ... the big monstrous
teddy bear that looks like you tried to draw all
your sad feelings ... *the Gorblimey*. How long
have you two been a 'thing'?"

"Uh, since last year," replied Ben. "But I didn't imagine anyone for ages after we – I mean, after you decided to stay in the old house."

"I didn't decide to stay, you decided to go without me," snapped Daisy. "You decided you didn't want to be 'Bad Ben' who answers back and starts fights and sets fires. You wanted to hide away like a big crybaby and do nothing with your life except arrange birthday parties that no one comes to."

Ben winced at the thought that Daisy had been there at the house, an invisible witness to yesterday's bizarre events (although technically it meant one more guest at his tragic party) – and then he remembered the words written on his wall.

"You blunted my pencils," Ben said as sternly as he could. "It was you, wasn't it?"

"Of course it was me – who else even knows

you exist?" Daisy sneered. "No one, that's who."

"I'm *telling* on you," said Ben, clenching his fists in frustration. "This is all your fault! I'm telling Mum and Dad what you did!"

"'Telling'? What are you, six?" Daisy replied. "You can't blame me for this, crybaby. You just said it yourself, I heard you – this is *your* fault. You made me – I'm all the bad things you ever did, and you wanted to forget that you ever did them. So you forgot me."

"I didn't!" Ben cried. "Is that why you're doing all this? 'Cause you think I forgot you?"

"You did forget me! You never came back! One minute you were there and the next you were gone," Daisy growled, her face flushing a dark grey as she looked Ben square in the eyes. "Well, now the Gorblimey has gone too – bounced all the way out of your life. Now *you* know what it's like to lose a friend."

"Daisy, I didn't forget," Ben said, tears welling in his eyes. "You were my friend but—"

"Pfff, like I'd want to be friends with you anyway," Daisy tutted. "I'm going to get a new friend – someone who's not a crybaby."

"Who?" Ben asked.

"Don't know yet," replied Daisy. The sight of her lopsided smile immediately made Ben nervous. "But I know where to look – Oblivion."

"What?" Ben said, his eyes wide. "H-how do you know about that?"

"I was here when this old bone-bag came knocking, you toenail – sitting in the fireplace, as invisible as farts," Daisy explained. She craned to look over her shoulder at Skeleton Keys' headless body. "Bone-bag was banging on about Oblivion, and I got to wondering who else he's locked in there, in that big prison of nothing ... who else has been forgotten? Then he said it – *'After what happened with your dad.'* And it hit me like an iron poker on the back of the head. It all makes sense..."

"What makes sense? What about my dad?" Ben asked. With everything that had happened, he'd almost forgotten Skeleton Keys' cryptic statement.

"Why do you think bone-bag was worried about the Gorblimey being dangerous? Just 'cause of his stupid twitch?" said Daisy with *that* smile. "Nah ... he's worried about history repeating itself. This is all about your *dad*, crybaby."

"I ... don't understand," Ben said. "Please, tell me..."

"You'll see," Daisy said. Her grin was replaced with a stranger expression. She looked like she wanted *revenge*. She leaned over Skeleton Keys' body and began inspecting each of his fingers in turn. "Now, which one was *the Key to Oblivion*? This one? This one? Aha! Here it is..."

Daisy grabbed the skeleton's right index finger and twisted sharply. With a CRACK the finger snapped clean off the hand. She held up the finger and peered at it.

"Daisy!" Ben cried. "Put that back!"

"Time to find my new friend," she said with a grin. Then, as she began to fade and disappear, she added, "After I'm finished, no one is going to forget me, ever again."

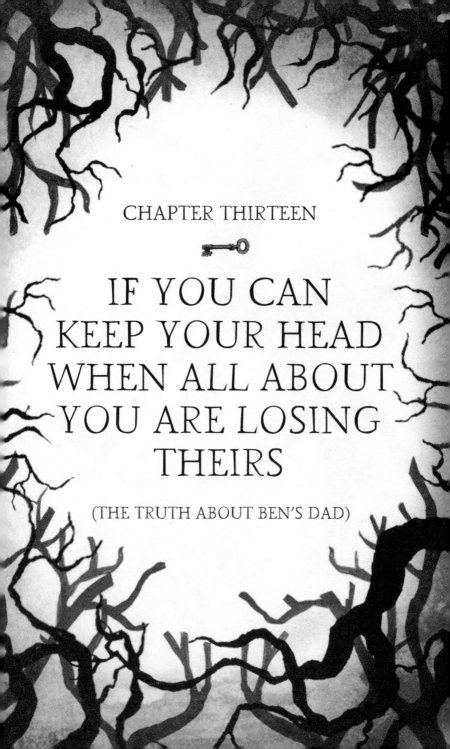

CHAPTER THIRTEEN

IF YOU CAN
KEEP YOUR HEAD
WHEN ALL ABOUT
YOU ARE LOSING
THEIRS

(THE TRUTH ABOUT BEN'S DAD)

"Life is what you make of it.
Unless someone else gets there first."
—SK

"Wait...!" muttered Ben as Daisy vanished. He stood there in the burned-out front room, dread and panic mounting as he stared down at the skull at his feet. Daisy was on the loose with *the Key to Oblivion* and the Gorblimey was gone.

Ben decided he should probably find his mum and dad, even if it meant getting in all sorts of trouble. He turned to go ... only to find his path blocked by a headless skeleton in a tailored suit.

Skeleton Keys' body was on its feet.

"AAAARGH!" Ben screamed as the skeleton lumbered towards him. Ben stumbled backwards, tripping over Skeleton Keys' head and toppling on to the soaked carpet. The skeleton loomed over him ... then bent down and picked up his head. The jaw of the skull swung and rattled as the skeleton pressed it on to his neck. Then with a sharp CLACK the head snapped into place.

"Where was I?" said Skeleton Keys. "Ah, yes – my twitch, lest we forget, is never wrong and— Wait, did someone knock my head off again?"

"You – you're alive!" cried Ben, scrambling to his feet.

"It takes more than having my head separated from my body to cramp Ol' Mr Keys' style," declared the skeleton. "Was it the Gorblimey? That fiend! Fret not, I shall—"

"No! I told you, it was Daisy! Daisy!" Ben wailed. "She's a girl with a backwards head who can turn invisible and hates everything and she's *unimaginary* now. *She* knocked your head off!"

"Daisy, you say?" he said. "Cheese 'n' biscuits, what a dangerous unimaginary she must be. I knew my skull-ache was right on the money – the twitch is never wrong…"

Ben slapped his palm against his forehead.

"*You got it all wrong* – all of it!" he yelled. "Now Daisy's gone and the Gorblimey's gone too!"

Skeleton Keys scratched his head, his fingers scraping noisily along his skull.

"I suppose I *might* have got the wrong end of the twitch, what with this Daisy of yours being invisible and— AiEE!" Skeleton Keys squealed as he spotted the bone stump where his little finger used to be.

"*And* she stole your finger after she knocked your head off," Ben explained.

"Dogs 'n' cats, she is a monster!" cried Skeleton Keys, inspecting his stump. "I have been after the wrong unimaginary this entire time! What a saddle-goose! I was just so desperate not to fail you, after everything that happened with your father..."

"What *did* happen?" insisted Ben, exasperated. "Daisy said my dad's the reason for *all* of this. What did she mean? Tell me!"

Skeleton Keys sighed. "Very well – but be warned, it is a hum-dum-dinger of a tale," he began. "Your father had an imaginary friend."

"What?" Ben gasped. "When? Who?"

"His name was Beardbeard the Pirate," Skeleton Keys continued. "Your father imagined him on the eve of his fifth birthday. Beardbeard was a formidable rugslugger – strong, fearless and, as it happened, thoroughly unpleasant. Imagine all the anger you have ever felt – every wild, squally, crunch-foot feeling that furrowed your brow and maddened your mind ... that was Beardbeard. He was nothing but trouble. Now, it is all very well having a trouble-chum when they only exist in your imagination but when they are suddenly as real as roof tiles, it can be an absolute flabbergaster! Sure enough, your father imagined his IF so well that he became unimaginary. But, when he laid eyes upon the unimagined Beardbeard, your father was terrified. He ran away in fear – ran and ran and did not stop running. Even I could not find him."

"He was scared?" Ben said. He couldn't imagine the Gorblimey being even slightly scary ... but there was no doubt that Daisy made him nervous.

"To badden matters, Beardbeard then summoned his great ship and went searching

for the one thing every pirate craves –
treasure," continued Skeleton Keys. "He
destroyed everything in his path, starting
with your grandparents' home. Beardbeard
reduced it to rubble and dust." Skeleton Keys
gazed at the space where his little finger used
to be. "I was left with no other choice..."

"*The Key to Oblivion*," said Ben, the penny
dropping as if in slow motion. "Is ... is that
what you did to Beardbeard the Pirate? Sent
him to Oblivion?"

"I had to end his rampage!" cried Skeleton
Keys. "Since Beardbeard was obsessed with
finding treasure, I tricked him into thinking
he would find it *inside* Oblivion. I opened
the door and the foolsome pirate disappeared
through it. In the moment he vanished, every
memory of Beardbeard vanished too. Your
father forgot him in an instant. He remembers
nothing of his IF, or that fateful day."

"But wait, *you* still remember," Ben said. "You put Beardbeard in Oblivion and you haven't forgotten him."

"Yes, well, I am rather a one-off," Skeleton Keys noted. "The problem is that while Oblivion erased your father's memories, it could not erase his *feelings*. I fear that losing his memory of Beardbeard the Pirate has tied your father's feelings in a bother-knot. He has spent his life looking for something he does not know he has lost."

Ben rubbed his eyes. Suddenly, his dad's obsession with the sea, his precious matchstick ship, the constant moving from coast to coast, island to island – it all started to make a strange sort of sense. All this time, Ben's dad was searching for his lost memories of Beardbeard the Pirate – even though he couldn't remember what he was searching for. Ben remembered Daisy's message – "You forgot me" – and a sudden sense of guilt began to turn his stomach. Maybe he *had* tried to forget her. Could he blame her for trying to find a new friend?

"But wait – Daisy said she was going to find a *new* friend," said Ben. "And now she has *the Key to Oblivion*. Do you think she's going to—"

"Swallow the key and run off to join the circus?" interrupted Skeleton Keys. "Just what I was thinking!"

"Or *maybe* she's going to open the door to Oblivion and free Beardbeard..." suggested Ben.

"Exactly what I was going to say!" declared Skeleton Keys. "Enough chin-waggering – we must find Daisy before she opens the door to Oblivion and releases Beardbeard!"

"But what about the Gorblimey?" asked Ben. "He's out there somewhere, all on his own…"

"Hat 'n' gloves, Benjamin, your friend must wait," declared Skeleton Keys. "Do you have any idea what might happen if Daisy releases Beardbeard?"

"No," confessed Ben.

"Last time, he destroyed your father's home. Why, he very nearly destroyed an entire town in search of his treasure. We must find Daisy before she uses that key," said Skeleton Keys. He rushed over to the chest of drawers, and with a *CLUNK-CLICK*, opened it to reveal a void of blackness. "That-a-way!" he cried, pointing inside the drawer. "Do not diddle-dally!"

"Where are we going…?" Ben asked.

"To the world of infinite doorways, of course," Skeleton Keys replied, clambering into the drawer. "To my Doorminion!"

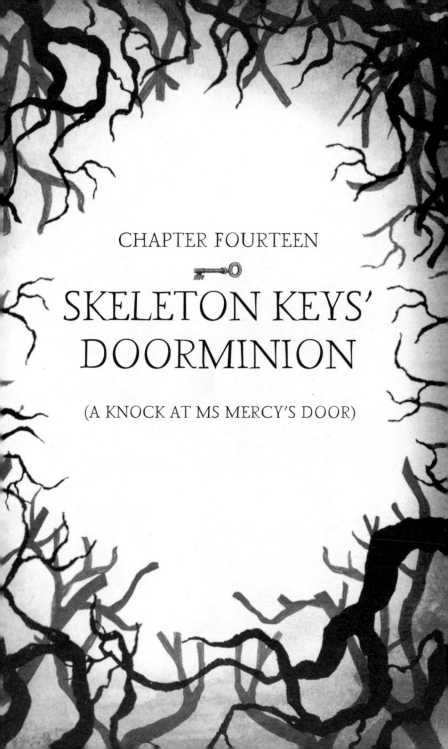

CHAPTER FOURTEEN

SKELETON KEYS' DOORMINION

(A KNOCK AT MS MERCY'S DOOR)

From *The Important Thoughts of Mr S. Keys*
Volume 2: The Key to Doorminion

Countless doors lead to countless adventures!

As Skeleton Keys disappeared into the
drawer, Ben looked out of the smashed
window and stared into the sky, hoping to see
the Gorblimey emerge through the clouds.
But his friend was well and truly gone.

"Please come back," he sighed. Then,
without a plan to find Daisy and no
better idea than following Skeleton Keys,
he clambered into the drawer. He was
immediately swallowed into the lightless
abyss and, as the drawer slammed shut above
his head, he felt himself start to fall...

"Aaaa–uff!" Ben wailed, landing suddenly on a cold, hard floor.

"Welcome to my Doorminion! Sorry about the mess, I was not expecting visitors," Skeleton Keys declared.

Ben stood up and looked around. There was no "mess" – Doorminion was a void of light-swallowing blackness. Ben would have no sense of distance or direction but for one thing – a seemingly infinite number of identical white doors, suspended in the darkness and stretching endlessly in every direction. It was the most dizzying sight he had ever seen.

"Where do they all go?" he asked.

"This-a-way, that-a-way ... they are the doors to all other doors," Skeleton Keys replied. "A world of entrances and exits ... and Daisy must be behind one of them."

"How about this one?" said Ben, pointing at the nearest door.

"You mean, of the near-infinite number of doors in my Doorminion, is Daisy behind the one that you *happen* to be standing next to?" scoffed Skeleton Keys. "Cheese 'n' biscuits, Benjamin, we cannot rely on guesswork and goose-ploys! I must use the *twitch*..."

"The twitch?" repeated Ben.

"My twitch is never stronger than here, in my Doorminion," explained Skeleton Keys. "With enough concentration and a half-decent headwind, I may be able to use the twitch to find Daisy, invisible or not."

"Wait, could you find the Gorblimey?"

Ben asked.

"Why would I want to find the Gorblimey? He is harmless! You must try and keep up, Benjamin — it is *Daisy* who is dangerous," said Skeleton Keys. Ben saw the skeleton's head shudder and jolt so quickly he thought it might fall off again. "Come out, come out, wherever you are..." he said, his teeth chattering as he spoke.

As Skeleton Keys entered a trance-like twitch-state, Ben paced up and down in the blackness. If Daisy was behind one of these doors, that meant the Gorblimey was too. He was out there somewhere, alone and probably scared out of his wits.

Ben glanced again at the nearest door. Despite himself, he reached out for the plain, round handle. He turned it and slowly pushed. The door opened with an ominous

CREEEAK.

The first thing he saw was the Chair of Doom outside the head teacher's office.

He was back in the corridor of his school.

Ben peeked around the other side of the Doorminion door, and saw the sign for the girls' toilet.

"No way…" he whispered. Through the window in her office, Ben could see Ms Mercy was on the phone. She was speaking in her "teacher voice", so even though her door was shut, Ben could hear every word.

"Doctor Bunsen? It's Marcy Mercy, Grundy Island Primary," she began.

She's talking to Mum! Ben thought, his heart in his mouth.

"I'm sorry to tell you that your son Benjamin has acquired … a *monster*," Ms Mercy continued. "Yes, I said 'monster'. Yes, I saw it! It jumped on to my desk!" Ms Mercy took off her glasses and rubbed her eyes. "If you don't mind me saying so, Doctor, you don't sound overly concerned. Well, I must inform you that I saw Benjamin and his monster climb out of my window and bounce off into the clouds! Truancy, Doctor Bunsen, is taken very seriously at this school, whether in the company of a monster or n—"

KNOCK.

KNOCK.

Ben heard the knock at her door but there was no one there to do the knocking. He froze.

"Excuse me, I must go," Ms Mercy said. She hung up the phone and opened her door. Ben ducked back into Skeleton Keys' Doorminion as the head strode out into the corridor and looked around. He kept the door open just a crack and heard Ms Mercy say, "Who did that? Who knocked?"

Ben heard her door slam shut. Then:

CLUNK-CLICK.

Ben dared to peek around the door again. Ms Mercy stood outside her office, inspecting her door. Something was sticking out of the lock.

It was Skeleton Keys' finger. *The Key to Oblivion.*

Oh no... Ben mouthed.

"Very funny! I know a *prank* when I see one," Ms Mercy declared loudly, reaching for the door handle. "It's going to take more than that to scare me – I had a monster on my desk half an hour ago..."

"Wait, don't!" cried Ben, rushing out into the corridor, but it was too late – Ms Mercy swung open her door. Her office had been replaced with a mass of swirling, glowing clouds as big as a hundred oceans. The angry, churning maelstrom spiralled into a deep vortex with a bright light at its centre. Ms Mercy stumbled backwards, her horrified scream echoing through the school corridors.

"That's for picking on the crybaby," said a voice as Daisy materialized in the corridor. "Nobody picks on him but *me*."

"Daisy!" cried Ben. "What did you do?"

"Crybaby? What are you doing here? Are you jealous 'cause I'm about to meet my new friend?" Daisy replied with a grin. She leaned into the swirling vortex

"Come out, come out, wherever you are..."

CHAPTER FIFTEEN

THE RETURN
OF BEARDBEARD

(DAISY'S NEW BEST FRIEND)

"Some unimaginaries are best forgotten."
—SK

"It's Daisy! It's Daisy!" cried Ben, racing back into the Doorminion.

"Dogs 'n' cats, I know who I am looking for," said Skeleton Keys. "But the longer you distract me, the longer it will take me to find—"

"I found her!" Ben cried, grabbing the skeleton by his coat-tails and dragging him back towards the door to the school.

"Wait, I am starting to sense something ... Daisy is close!" declared Skeleton Keys as Ben pushed him through the door into the school corridor. "We must stop her before she uses *the Key to— Ah.*"

Skeleton Keys was confronted with the sight of Daisy peering into the swirling maelstrom of Oblivion.

"You haven't come here to stop me, have you? "'Cause you two are too late," she said, looking back at them (or literally forwards since she had a backwards head). "But you're just in time to meet my new best friend..."

"YARRB!"

From the churning vortex emerged a mountain of a man. He was twice as tall as Ben's dad and broad as a wall, with girder-thick arms and legs. What little of his face was visible was so weather-beaten and craggy it looked more like a cliff face than an actual face. The bottom half of it was dominated by not one but *two* beards. An entire, jet-black beard grew out of the right side of his face while a fiery red beard sprouted from the left. The pirate had two curved golden hooks instead of hands, and two wooden pegs in place of legs. He completed his look with a long coat, cuffed boots, and a hat so wide-brimmed that it made a whistling sound when he turned his head.

"*Crumcrinkles*," cursed Skeleton Keys. "Beardbeard has returned!"

"SHIBBERY TIMBERS! I BE BEARDBEARD THE PIRATE!"

Beardbeard bellowed, his voice a deafening boom.

At the sight of the giant, two-of-everything pirate, Ben gasped. Despite looking and sounding fairly ridiculous, Beardbeard sent cold, paralyzing dread coursing through Ben's body. It was all he could do not to run – run and hide, just like his dad had done all those years ago.

"My new best friend is bigger than yours," noted Daisy, enjoying Ben's fear as he stared up in horror at the pirate striding into the corridor.

"BRING ME THE TREASURE!" Beardbeard roared, raising a hook aloft. "I BE WANTIN' THE TREASURE!"

"OK, he's a bit loud ... I can live with that," said Daisy, wincing at the din. She turned to Beardbeard and added, "Maybe you should let *me* do the talk—"

"TREASURE! WHERE BE THE TREASURE?" boomed Beardbeard. "I MUST BE FINDIN' THE TREASURE!"

"Yeah, I heard you the first time you shouted *right in my ear*," huffed Daisy. "Y'know, I didn't free you so you could just yell about treasure. You're supposed to be dangerous. If you're going to be my best friend you'd better start—"

"YOU!" the pirate hollered, pointing a hook at Skeleton Keys. "YOU BE THE CURVY DOG WHO LOCKED ME IN THAT SWIRLIN' WORLD O' NOTHIN' AND KEPT ME FROM THE TREASURE!"

"B-Beardbeard! H-how long has it been?"
said a panicking Skeleton Keys as the pirate
rounded on him. "Now, you should know
that I was *certain* that I'd never see you again
after banishing you to Oblivion, so if anyone
is the victim here, it is m— AKK!"

Before Skeleton Keys knew what was
happening, Beardbeard had struck. His golden
hook-hand locked around the skeleton's neck.

"That's more like it!" noted an impressed
Daisy.

"I – AKK! – do not want to sound
fussnickity," wheezed the skeleton, "but you
seem to have got my neck snagged on your –
URK! – hook..."

"YOU BE COMIN' WITH ME,
SKULLERTON – I BE MAKIN'
YOU WALK THE PLANK," growled
the pirate. He hoisted Skeleton Keys into the
air and bopped him hard on the head with

his other hook. In an instant, Skeleton Keys went limp.

"No…!" Ben cried.

"*Fine*, we can take the skeleton with us – but from now on you have to run all decisions past me," huffed Daisy. "Now, are we going to get this party started, or what?"

"AYE! LET'S BE FINDIN' THE TREASURE!" Beardbeard boomed, flinging the unconscious Skeleton Keys over his shoulder. Then he strode down the corridor with a *CLACK-CLOCK-CLACK* of wooden legs – and smashed through the wall like it was polystyrene.

"Try not to be jealous … even though he's a *lot* taller than you," Daisy sneered at Ben, before racing after the pirate with a "Wait for me!".

Ben suddenly remembered the head teacher, Ms Mercy, and turned to see her crouched against the wall and gazing, dumbfounded, into Oblivion's swirling vortex. If even *she* was terrified, how could he be expected to be brave?

Ben quickly slammed the door. He stared at Skeleton Keys' finger, hanging out of the lock, and decided he was so far out of his depth that the best and wisest and safest thing to do was absolutely *nothing*.

But a moment later, Ben plucked Skeleton Keys' finger out of the door and chased after Daisy.

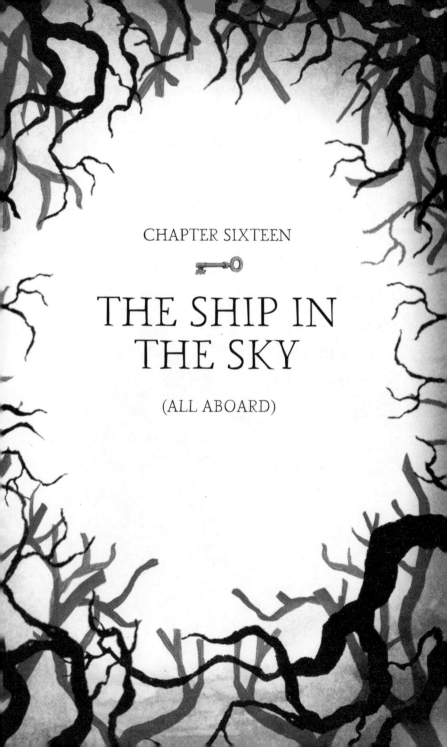

CHAPTER SIXTEEN

THE SHIP IN THE SKY

(ALL ABOARD)

Ben slipped Skeleton Keys' finger into his trouser pocket and raced through the hole at the end of the corridor. The day had grown grey and heavy with fog. Ben spotted Beardbeard with Skeleton Keys still slung over his shoulder. With great, clopping strides the pirate had already reached the other end of the car park but Daisy, with her awkward, backwards walk, was finding it harder to navigate the sea of cars. Ben quickly caught up with her and grabbed her by the arm.

"Daisy, stop!" he said in a desperate

whisper. "We've got to get Beardbeard back into Oblivion!"

"Get lost, crybaby," Daisy snarled. "Beardbeard's my best friend now – you and me are finished."

"I don't care about— Beardbeard is *dangerous*, Daisy!" replied Ben. "Skeleton Keys said he nearly blew up a whole town!"

"Now *that* I'd like to see. How did he do it?" said Daisy. As if on cue, Beardbeard flung his arms into the air and roared so loudly it set off three car alarms.

"AHOY, ME HARD CHEESE! I'LL BE NEEDIN' ME SHIP TO HELP WITH THE TREASURE GETTIN'!"

The pirate reached a hook into his coat and pulled out a small model of a pirate ship. Ben stared in disbelief – the ship looked almost identical to the model his dad had made from matchsticks.

"I BE NEEDIN' YOU SHIPSHAPE, SHIP!" the pirate bellowed, flinging the ship high into the air. As it flew skywards, the ship began to *grow*. Within seconds, Ben could see a full-size galleon beyond the haze of fog. It floated above them, casting a dark shadow over the whole school.

The ship's vast, skull-covered sails whipped and snapped in the breeze, and twenty or more cannons protruded from openings in the hull.

"So, it turns out my new best friend is the owner-operator of a flying pirate ship," said Daisy, peering upwards with that lopsided grin on her grey face. "Where's *your* best friend again? Oh yeah, he ran away."

"A VAST TEA! TIME TO SELL SAIL! DROP THE ANGER!" boomed Beardbeard. He clanged his hooks together and an anchor as big as the pirate himself plummeted towards the ground on a thick iron chain. Ben leaped out of the way as it ploughed into the car park. "THERE BE TREASURE TO BE FINDIN'!" roared Beardbeard. He locked both hooks into the links of the chain and, with Skeleton Keys still slung over his shoulder, began to climb up and up until he reached his flying ship.

"Right, I'm off! Me and BB – I call him BB – have got stuff to do…" said Daisy. "Don't feel bad that you don't even *have* a— Hey!"

The sound of shattering tarmac filled the air as the ship's anchor started moving, dragged along the ground by its chain. Daisy looked up.

The ship was leaving.

"Oi! Beardbeard, wait for me!" Daisy screamed. She raced down the street as the anchor was wrenched out of the ground and began to withdraw into the pirate ship. Daisy leaped on to the anchor and held on for dear life. "Come back! You forgot me!"

"Daisy!" shouted Ben, racing after the pirate ship as the anchor dragged Daisy up into the sky. Without thinking, he leaped into the air and grabbed on to Daisy's legs.

"Leave me alone, you smelly sock!" Daisy howled.

"No! I'm not going anywhere!" cried Ben. True to his word, Ben did not let go of Daisy. The anchor's chain hoisted the pair up and up until they were pulled inside the bowels of Beardbeard's ship. Ben outraced Daisy up a flight of creaky wooden stairs and through an equally creaky door to find himself on the deck. He quickly ducked behind a stack of barrels.

"Where's Skeleton Keys?" Ben whispered to himself, peeking out. Beardbeard's ship was an imposing sight. The long wooden deck stretched as far as he could see and smelled faintly of fish. Ben glanced up. Directly above the creaky door was another smaller deck, with stairs leading up to it on both sides. On this quarter deck stood Beardbeard at the ship's wheel. Skeleton Keys' limp body still hung over his shoulder. Ben watched the pirate pluck the skeleton up with a hook and, with a loud clatter of bones, cast him on to the deck.

"THERE BE ONLY ONE WAY TO FIND THE TREASURE!" declared Beardbeard. "BLASTIN' EVERYTHIN' TO BITS 'N' PIECES!"

With a BOOM! BOOM! BOOM! BOOM! cannonballs streaked out from the ship towards the ground. Ben covered his ears as the first salvo obliterated the number twenty-eight bus stop, blasted Grundy Island pier to rubble and reduced Mr Pinchpenny's casino to dust.

He's destroying the island! Mum! Dad! Ben thought in horror. *I have to get to Skeleton Keys ... I have to find a way to distract Beardbeard so I can—*

"Oi! Pirate!" Daisy howled, appearing in the doorway at the top of the creaky stairs. Ben whispered, "Daisy!", but she either didn't hear him or chose to ignore him. Either way, she walked up the steps to the quarter deck and tugged at Bearbeard's long coat. "You left without me!" she cried. "You forgot me!"

The pirate leaned towards her, his great
beards swaying like trees in the wind.

"WHO BE YOU?" he asked.

"Who be me? I be Daisy!" she replied, her
hands on her hips. "I'm the one who just
freed you from Oblivion, remember? You and
me are best friends!"

"BEARDBEARD HAS NO NEED OF YOU," scoffed the pirate. "BEARDBEARD NEEDS ONLY THE TREASURE."

"Yeah, well, you still have to do what I say – that's what being a friend means," Daisy insisted, but Beardbeard returned to his wheel. "Hey, I'm talking to you!"

"Daisy, don't...!" Ben hissed from behind the barrel but Daisy spun round and kicked one of Beardbeard's wooden legs as hard as she could.

"If it wasn't for me you'd still be stuck in Oblivion and no one would even remember that they forgot you!" Daisy roared. "Now, do as you're told, or else!"

"I COULD BE DOING THAT," said Beardbeard, thoughtfully stroking both beards with his hooks. Then suddenly the pirate struck, skewering the back of Daisy's dress and lifting her into the air. "OR I COULD JUST BE THROWIN' YOU OVERBOARD..."

CHAPTER SEVENTEEN

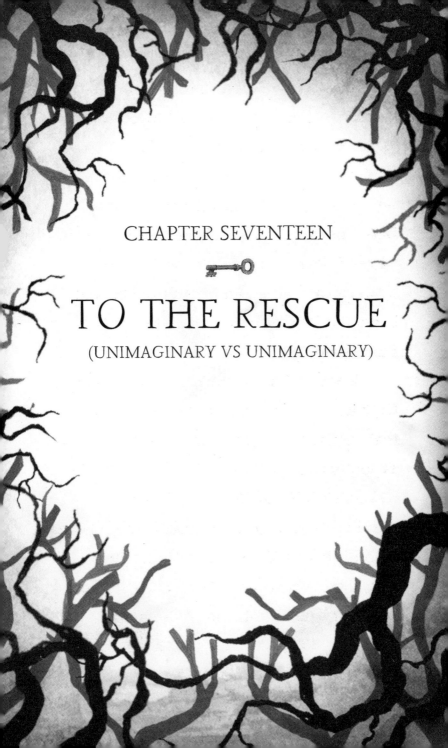

TO THE RESCUE

(UNIMAGINARY VS UNIMAGINARY)

From *The Important Thoughts of Mr S. Keys*
Volume 14: Unimaginaries Through the Ages

*UNIMAGINARY PIRATES I WOULD BE GADDLY
GLADDENED NEVER TO MEET AGAIN*
Blackbeard
Goldenbeard
Ironbeard
NoBeard
Beardbeard

"Don't you dare overboard me!" cried Daisy, struggling in vain as Beardbeard dangled her over the edge of the ship.

"Hey!" came a cry. "Let go of my friend!"

The pirate looked down to see Ben racing up the stairs to the quarter deck.

"ANOTHER STOWAWAY?" growled Beardbeard. "AND WHO BE YOU BE, LAND BLUBBER?"

"I be ... I'm B-Ben," Ben replied, trying to sound brave but squeaking like a mouse.

"And ... and that's my friend."

"Really?" murmured Daisy. "You mean it?"

"Of course ... you'll *always* be my friend," said Ben, smiling weakly at Daisy despite being pant-wettingly scared. He slowly turned back to Beardbeard. "Now, p-please leave Daisy alone."

"I COULD BE DOING THAT ... OR I COULD JUST BE THROWIN' YOU *BOTH* OUT!" growled Beardbeard. Ben's panic doubled as the pirate swung his other hook, piercing Ben's sweater and hoisting him into the air.

"YOU BE A PAIN IN MY BEARDS," cried Beardbeard, dangling them both off the edge of the ship. "HAPPY LANDIN'S, YOU LAND BLU—"

PooOOoM!

Beardbeard was thrown backwards, toppling over the ship's wheel and plummeting to the deck below. He threw his arms wide, and Ben and Daisy were flung from his hooks, skidding and skittering along the hard wooden floor. Ben's head spun as he looked up and saw a dark shape looming over him.

It was the Gorblimey.

"Gorblimey! You came back!" Ben cried, leaping up and throwing his arms around the monster. The Gorblimey purred, his candle flame glowing a deep orange, and squeezed Ben so hard it left him breathless.

"Where did you go? How did you find me?" Ben wheezed. He understood the Gorblimey's hooting reply perfectly – the monster had never dared bounce further than the end of their street. What's more, the sudden appearance of a giant flying pirate ship had convinced him that Ben may well need his help.

"I *really* did," said Ben, breathing a sigh of relief. The Gorblimey gave a final, quizzical honk. "Of *course* I think you're brave!" Ben replied, hugging his friend back with all his might.

"Crybabies," huffed Daisy as she folded her arms.

"CURVY DOG!" Beardbeard snarled as he got to his feet. The Gorblimey put himself between Ben and the pirate and growled like a dog guarding a bone. "I'LL BE TEACHIN' YOU TO GET BETWEEN A PIRATE AND HIS TREASURE!" Beardbeard bellowed.

"Don't fight him, Gorblimey, he's dangerous!" cried Ben as the monster and the pirate squared off against each other. "And he's got two of everything!"

"Get him, Beardbeard!" yelled Daisy as Beardbeard rounded on the Gorblimey. "Teach that fat teddy bear a lesson!"

"Whose side are you on, Daisy?" shouted Ben. "Beardbeard was going to throw you off the ship! If he wins, we're all going overboard!"

"Fair point," Daisy admitted. "Kick that pirate's beards in, Gorblimey!"

The Gorblimey ducked as Beardbeard swung his hooks wildly, letting out fearful honks as the pirate's strikes got closer and closer...

"Shrink, Gorblimey! Shrink and hide!" cried Ben. The Gorblimey tooted in agreement and immediately shrank to pocket-size, all but disappearing in front of Beardbeard's face.

"WHERE BE HE?" the pirate growled as the tiny Gorblimey darted behind a crate. Beardbeard began scouring the deck, *click-clacking* to and fro on his peg legs. "WHERE BE YOU, CURVY DOG? COME OUT AND FACE ME!"

"Daisy, now's our chance! Let's get ... Daisy?" said Ben, looking around. Daisy had vanished again. Ben let out a frustrated grunt before scampering up the stairs to the quarter deck. By the time he'd reached the limp body of Skeleton Keys, Ben could hear Beardbeard tearing his own ship apart in search of the Gorblimey.

"Skeleton— Mr Keys!" Ben said in an urgent whisper, shaking the skeleton by his shoulders. "Wake up! You have to wake—"

"Crumcrinkles!" yelped Skeleton Keys, sitting bolt upright. He shook his head and checked his fingers. "Benjamin, *please* tell me you have *the Key to Oblivion*."

"The what? Oh, yes!" said Ben, digging in his pocket and pulling out the skeleton's finger. Skeleton Keys pressed his finger to the socket on his hand and rolled it until it stuck.

"Much better – I do so hate having fewer than all two hundred and six bones," he said. "Now then, any chance there is a door around here?"

"There's one right below us!" Ben told him. They both peered over the ship's wheel to see Beardbeard tearing up the deck with his hooks. "What are you going to do?"

"Something I should have done a long time ago ... actually, the exact same thing I *did* do a long time ago," said Skeleton Keys dramatically. "I only hope that hook-handed, wood-footed flabbergaster is as witless as I remember..."

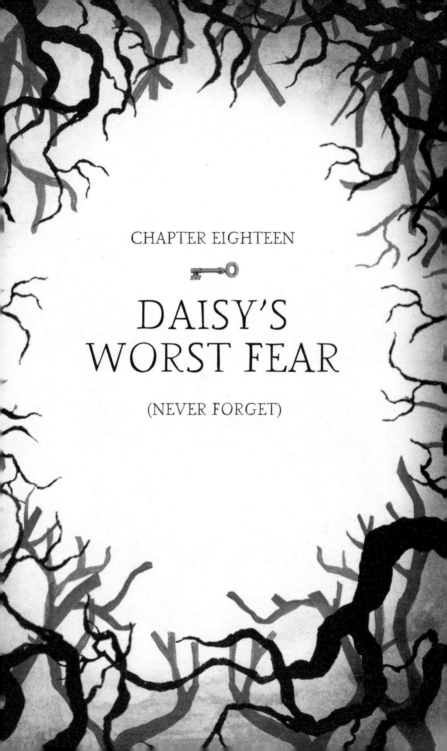

CHAPTER EIGHTEEN

DAISY'S
WORST FEAR

(NEVER FORGET)

"A true friend, however imaginary,
is never forgotten."
—SK

Ben watched Skeleton Keys vault over the ship's wheel to the deck below. He slipped his finger into the creaky door. With a *CLUNK-CLICK* he swung it open, to reveal the churning, swirling world of Oblivion.

"Beardbeard!" Skeleton Keys cried as the pirate continued his mad search for the Gorblimey. "I have found the treasure!"

"THE TREASURE? IT'S MINE!" roared the pirate. He spun round to see Skeleton Keys gesturing pointedly at the door to Oblivion.

"What giddy-gaddling luck!" declared Skeleton Keys. "Look, the treasure was on your ship the whole time!"

"WAIT, BE THAT NOT THE DOOR TO THE SWIRLIN' WORLD O' NOTHIN' I JUST CAME FROM?" said Beardbeard suspiciously. "IT BE LOOKING VERY SIMILAR..."

"This? Oh my, no!" declared Skeleton Keys, feigning surprise. "This is an entirely *different* swirling world of nothing. And it is absolutely cram-bursting with treasure! All you have to do is step inside..."

From behind the ship's wheel, Ben found himself crossing his fingers, convinced that Beardbeard was about to separate Skeleton Keys into his individual bones.

But then:

"YES! THE TREASURE BE THROUGH THAT DOOR!" roared the pirate with glee. He began *CLACK-CLOCK*ing towards it with ever increasing speed. Ben slapped his hand over his mouth to stop himself from laughing. It was working. In seconds Beardbeard would throw himself into Oblivion. It would be over.

"Oi, pirate!"

At the cry, Daisy suddenly reappeared on the deck in front of the door. "I've decided this isn't working out!" she growled. "You and me, we're not best friends any more!"

Ben's momentary relief turned back to horror. Daisy was so hell-bent on scolding Beardbeard she hadn't realized Skeleton Keys' plan. She was blocking Beardbeard's path to the door – and the pirate wasn't stopping.

"Daisy, move!" wailed Ben as the pirate stormed towards her.

"OUT OF MY WAY!" Beardbeard bellowed. "I MUST BE GETTIN' THE TREASURE!"

"*Shut up* about treasure!" yelled Daisy. "I'm

talking! Me!" With that, she leaped on to one of Beardbeard's wooden legs (which isn't easy when your head and body point in different directions) and started climbing up his coat. She grabbed on to one of his two beards and clung on for dear life. "Don't ignore me!" she howled. "Don't you dare forget me!"

"Daisy, let go! He's not stopping!" Ben screamed, but Daisy wasn't listening. In a moment, Beardbeard would stride through the door into Oblivion, taking Daisy with him. Everyone – including Ben – would instantly lose all memory of her; she would be well and truly forgotten.

Daisy's worst fear would come true.

"No...!" Ben said to himself. What he did next surprised even him. He leaped over the quarter deck and landed – not softly – on top of Skeleton Keys. The pair collapsed in a heap of boy and bones but before the skeleton knew what had happened, Ben had scrambled to his feet and, with both hands, pushed the door to Oblivion shut.

"Benjamin, what have you done?" cried Skeleton Keys, still sprawled out on the deck. "Beardbeard was falling for my sneakish ploy all over again!"

"THE TREASURE!" roared Beardbeard madly. With Daisy still clinging to his beard, he tore the door from its hinges, to find a dim and disappointing stairwell down to the bowels of the ship. Beardbeard loomed over them and raised his hooks in rage.

"WHERE BE THE TREASURE? WHAT HAVE YOU DONE WITH THE TR— OWW!"

Beardbeard reeled as Daisy, who had burrowed into his bright copper beard, started pulling on his hair with all her might. Ben heard her shrieking and snarling from inside.

"Try and forget me now, you smelly sock!
I'll pull *both* your beards out!"

"That is our cue!" Skeleton Keys cried. He
wasted no time in grabbing Ben and ducking

underneath the pirate's legs. The skeleton raced along the deck towards the ship's bow.

"I'm sorry!" Ben said as Skeleton Keys dragged him along. "I couldn't let Beardbeard take Daisy into Oblivion! I can't let her be forgotten!"

"An admirable sentiment but that was the only door on deck!" said the skeleton.

"I know! I'm sorry!" Ben replied. He glanced back to see Beardbeard wrestling with his own facial hair as Daisy tried to tear it out.

"Well, you may have a point – I can hardly correct the mistakes of my past by repeating them in the present," admitted Skeleton Keys as they neared the front of the ship. "But if Beardbeard will not stop until he has found his treasure and we have no clue as to where his treasure is, then how— Wait. *Treasure!*"

Skeleton Keys skidded to a halt.

"What is it?" Ben asked.

"Dogs 'n' cats, could it be?" the skeleton mused, tapping his key-shaped fingertips against his chin. "Could it be that the treasure is actually— UFF!"

Skeleton Keys crumpled to the floor as Daisy struck him like a missile. Beardbeard had launched her through the air, having finally wrenched her from inside his beards.

"You missing something, pirate?" Daisy laughed, scrambling to her feet clutching a fistful of black beard hair in one hand and red hair in the other.

As Skeleton Keys reeled with another skull-ache, Ben turned to see Beardbeard *CLACK-CLOCK*ing across the deck towards them.

"THERE BE TWO THINGS I BE HATIN' IN LIFE – UNFOUND TREASURE AND UNFINISHED BUSINESS," growled the pirate, raising his hooks to strike. "OVERBOARD BE TOO GOOD FOR YOU LAND BLUBBERS.

I THINK I'LL JUST BE SQUASHIN' YOU LIKE FLIES..."

Ben closed his eyes, too scared to see what was coming ... but then he heard a familiar, high-pitched whistling sound.

"Gorblimey?" Ben cried as the monster appeared in front of him, growing to full size in an instant. Before Beardbeard could strike, the Gorblimey scooped up Ben and Daisy in his arms. Ben grabbed Skeleton Keys tightly by the leg and held on, before

PoOOooM!

"I'LL BE FINDIN' YOU, LAND BLUBBERS!" roared Beardbeard as the Gorblimey soared through the clouds. "AND THEN I'LL BE FINDIN' THE TREASURE ... BUT FIRST I'LL BE FINDIN' YOU!"

"Hat 'n' gloves, what a rescue!" declared Skeleton Keys, dangling by the leg as Ben held him tightly. "I apologize for ever accusing you of being a beastly ne'er do well!"

The Gorblimey cooed with delight, his candle flame glowing brightly.

"Yeah, well, I wasn't finished giving that pirate a piece of my mind," complained Daisy. "He probably still thinks we're best friends, the big crybaby..."

Ben glanced back to see Beardbeard's ship changing course to pursue them. "You might get your chance – he's coming after us! What do we do?"

"We take him to the treasure," replied Skeleton Keys. "That-a-way, Gorblimey! Bounce that-a-way!"

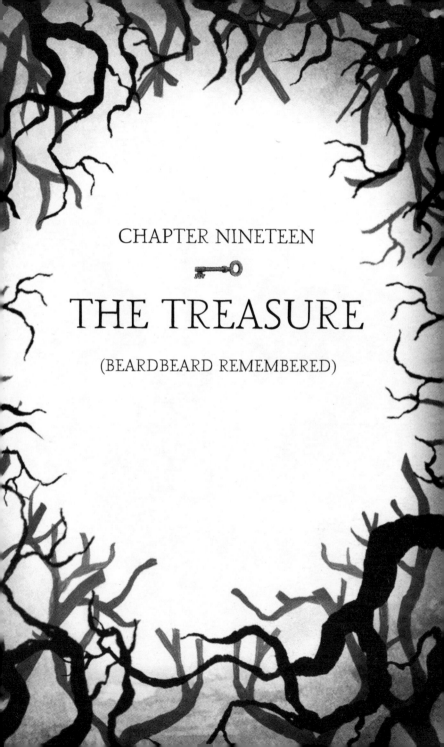

CHAPTER NINETEEN

THE TREASURE

(BEARDBEARD REMEMBERED)

From *The Important Thoughts of Mr S. Keys*
Volume 10: The Key to Oblivion

INSTRUCTIONS: *Only to be used in case of*
Unimaginably Unmanageable Unimaginary

Skeleton Keys directed the Gorblimey to bounce everyone to the northernmost tip of the island.

Ben did not realize until they landed where the skeleton had brought them.

The first thing he noticed was a small wooden windmill. Then a number of tiny bridges and tunnels and flags, and finally a large sign hung from a pole, which read:

GRUNDY ISLAND CRAZY GOLF
You don't have to be crazy to golf here,
but it helps!

They'd landed in the middle of his dad's miniature golf course.

"What are we doing here? I thought you said Dad was terrified of Beardbeard!" Ben cried. "Gorblimey, bounce us out of here!"

"Hold your horseshoes, Benjamin," said Skeleton Keys. "I have a nagging in my skull that tells me the treasure may have been under our nose-holes all along."

"If it's buried under the golf course, I'm not digging it up," huffed Daisy. "But I still want my share."

A moment later, Ben's dad emerged from his office, a small wooden hut on the edge of the golf course.

"Ben? Ben!" he cried. "What are you doing h— AAAAARGH!"

For a moment, Ben thought his dad was screaming at the sight of Skeleton Keys. Then a dark shadow fell over the golf course as

Beardbeard's vast pirate ship emerged from the clouds. Ben saw his dad's eyes grow wide. He stood there, frozen in terror as he peered up at the ship.

"C-can't be," whimpered Ben's dad as the ship's anchor plunged towards them, shattering the miniature windmill and driving itself into the ground. Beardbeard descended from his ship, clambering down the anchor's chain before landing with a thud.

"SHIBBERY TIMBERS, I HAVE YOU NOW!" hollered the pirate, striding towards them on his wooden legs. "AND WHEN I HAVE SQUASHED YOU LIKE FLIES, I'LL BE FINDIN' ... THE ... TREASURE...?"

Beardbeard trailed off and slowed to a standstill. He dropped his hooks by his side and gazed at Ben's dad, a sudden, less-than ferocious expression upon his face.

"THE – THE TREASURE," said Beardbeard, his booming voice cracking with emotion. "AFTER ALL THESE YEARS, I HAVE FOUND YOU."

"Wait, what?" exclaimed Ben. He glanced over at his dad and saw the very last thing he expected – a smile, spread across his face.

"I remember … I remember you," Ben's dad said, gazing up at Beardbeard in wonder. "I *imagined* you. The dread pirate Beardbeard … two beards … two hooks … two wooden legs! Then, suddenly, you were *real*. You came out of the ocean…"

"*Unimaginary*," whispered Ben.

"But when I saw you, when I *actually* saw you," continued Ben's dad, "I was scared."

"'TIS UNDERSTANDABLE," said Beardbeard. "I BE AN INTIMIDATIN' SIGHT."

"I ran," continued Ben's dad. "I was so scared, I ran away."

"AND I BLEW UP EVERYTHIN' TRYIN' TO FIND YOU," said Beardbeard, with a tear in his eye.

"But then as soon as you were there, you were gone. All I remember is ... not being able to remember you," Ben's dad said. Skeleton Keys sheepishly rubbed the back of his skull. "I couldn't even remember what I'd been scared of ... I couldn't remember anything. I just knew something was missing."

"I BE SORRY IT HAS TAKEN ME SO LONG TO FIND YOU," said Beardbeard. "BUT I BE HERE NOW."

"I'm sorry too," Ben's dad replied. "I think I might have spent my whole life searching for you."

"SOME TREASURE BE HARD TO FIND," said the pirate. "BUT THAT BE THE BEST TREASURE OF ALL."

"Wait, Ben's *dad* is your precious treasure?"

groaned Daisy, glowering at Beardbeard.

"Ugh, you're the worst pirate ever."

"Skeleton— Mr Keys?" whispered Ben. "What's going on?"

"Treasure, Benjamin," the skeleton replied as he breathed a long sigh of relief. "Treasure comes in all shapes and sizes."

A moment later, Ben had to check with the Gorblimey that he was seeing what he was seeing – his dad and Beardbeard, hugging like old friends. Ben edged nervously towards them.

"Uh, Dad...?" Ben whispered, tapping his dad on the leg. "Beardbeard just tried to kill us."

"He did?" said Ben's dad, looking up at his unimaginary friend. "Is that true, Beardbeard?"

"AYE AYE, I DID BE DOIN' THAT," Beardbeard admitted. "BUT IT WAS ON ACCOUNT OF MY BEIN' IMAGINED AS A MAD AND PLUNDEROUS PIRATE. I BE

TRYIN' VERY HARD NOT TO DO THAT SORT OF THING ANY MORE."

"See? He'll try not to do it any more," said Ben's dad. He gave Ben a hug, and looked back at the trio of unimaginary friends behind them. "I don't know how this happened but ... thank you, *all* of you. Thank you for finding my friend."

"I did all the hard work," Daisy said. "These idiots just got in the way."

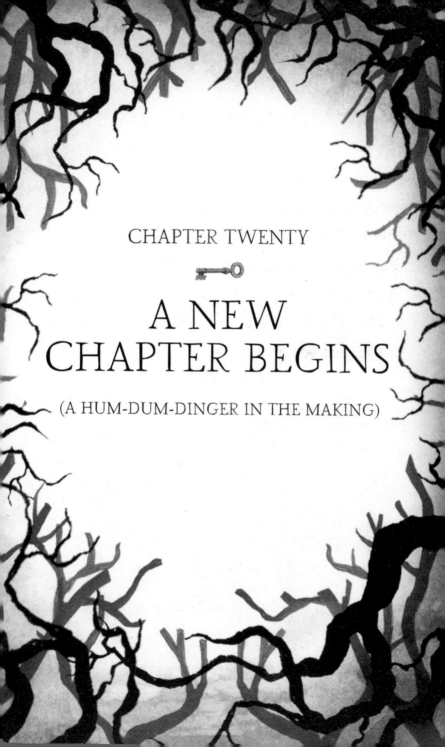

CHAPTER TWENTY

A NEW
CHAPTER BEGINS

(A HUM-DUM-DINGER IN THE MAKING)

From *Ol' Mr Keys Unimaginable Adventures, No. 1,001
– Ben's Unimaginary Friend*

*Ben faced a pirate, Soared the skies
Met danger! Thrilling spills! Surprise!
He learned that treasure is a friend
For treasured friendships never end.
Now, by my bones, I do declare
That Benjamin has friends to spare!*

"We're going to need a bigger dinner table," said Ben's mum. After an eventful couple of days, the Bunsens had decided to hold Ben's birthday party all over again. The front room might have been burned-out and flooded but at least this time they had guests. Everyone gathered for what little was left of Ben's birthday cake. It was a bit of a tight squeeze, trying to fit all three of them round the table plus the Gorblimey, Daisy, Beardbeard the Pirate and Skeleton Keys.

Ben couldn't have imagined a better party.
One day, he thought, he might like some
actual *people* to come (his mum and dad
didn't really count) – but for now, Ben's

unimaginary friends would do just fine. He
wouldn't have changed a thing.

"One piece of cake left – who wants it?"
asked Ben's mum.

"Me, obviously," huffed Daisy, holding out her hand and craning to see how big the slice was.

"YOU BE NEEDIN' TO LEARN SOME MANNERS, DAISY," tutted Beardbeard, dabbing his beards with a hanky knotted to one of his hooks. "POLITENESS BE COSTIN' NOTHING."

"Politeness?" Daisy scoffed. "You almost killed us!"

"And he apologized," said Ben's dad, waggling his finger at Daisy. "If I can forgive you for blowing up my ship, Daisy, you can let Beardbeard off a bit of *almost*-killing."

The Gorblimey let out a loud honk and Ben laughed. Then, even though no one else understood what the Gorblimey had said, they all laughed too.

"I'm not sure I'll ever get used to all this but it's already hard to imagine anything else," said Ben's mum, shaking her head.

"Crumcrinkles, is that the time? I must be away!" said Skeleton Keys, staring at his bony wrist. "It has been a pleasure knowing you all – although it would be ever so grinnering if you lot could stay out of trouble for a while. I am sure I shall have enough on my plate without you keeping me on my toe-bones..."

With that, he stood up from the table and made his way over to the chest of drawers. With a *CLUNK-CLICK* he opened a doorway to his Doorminion.

"Oi, hang on, bone-bag! I'm coming too," said Daisy, hopping down from her chair.

"Wait, *what?*" cried Ben and Skeleton Keys together.

"You didn't really think I was going to stay here, did you?" continued Daisy. "Look around – you lot are as happy as mucky pigs and everything's turned out fine. Even

Beardbeard's as soft as a kitten now he's found his 'treasure'. But not me – I like trouble, and the old bone-bag goes *looking* for it. I'm going to tag along for a while."

"Daisy, are you sure?" Ben asked. "You know you can stay with us. I meant what I said – I'll always be your friend, and I'll never forget you."

"Obviously not, I'm *unforgettable*," replied Daisy with a tut. After a moment she added, "But thanks for reminding me ... crybaby."

"I hate to be a bother-knot but do I not get a say in this?" asked Skeleton Keys.

"Nope," said Daisy, pushing past him to get to the drawer. "And from now on, maybe you should let *me* do the talking..." She looked back at Ben for just a moment, and then hopped into the drawer and disappeared. Skeleton Keys let out a long sigh.

"Crumcrinkles, why not? Perhaps even

Ol' Mr Keys could do with a friend," he said, throwing his arms in the air. "Very well then! A new tale begins – the adventures of Skeleton Keys and Daisy. A hum-dum-dinger in the making..."

With that, the skeleton disappeared into his Doorminion, and the drawer slammed shut.

S o there we have it, dallywanglers! The truly unbelievable, unbelievably true tale of Ben's unimaginary friends.

Did I not tell you it was a hum-dum-dinger? Action, intrigue, suspense and just enough hugging to remind us there is good in the world.

Of course, I did end up lumbered with Daisy. I cannot pretend it has been a butter-smooth ride thus far – she has a *lot* of demands, and does tend to set fire to my shoes – but I do believe her heart is in the right place … even if her head is facing the wrong way.

Well, Ol' Mr Keys' work is never done – I already feel another twitch in my bones. Who knows where it will lead? Perhaps to a tale so truly unbelievable that it must, unbelievably, be true. For it has been said, and it cannot be denied, that strange things can happen when imaginations run wild...

Until next time, until next tale, farewell!

Your servant in storytelling,

—SK

WANT TO FIND OUT ABOUT
SKELETON KEYS' NEXT ADVENTURE?

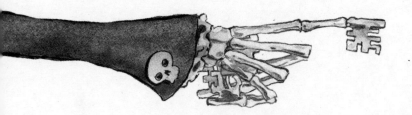

TURN THE PAGE TO FIND OUT...

Greetings! To waffleboggers, figswindlers and joustabouts! To the imaginary and the unimaginary! To the living, the dead and everyone in between, my name is Keys ... Skeleton Keys.

A long time ago and not at all recently, I was an IF – an imaginary friend. But by some wonder of wild imagining, I suddenly became as real as sticks! I had become unimaginary. Now, with these fantabulant fingers I can open doors to anywhere – hidden worlds ... secret places ... doors to the limitless realm of the imagination.

Today, I keep a watchful eye socket upon the recently unimagined wherever they appear. And each unimagining has led to an adventure that would make a head spin from its neck! The stories I could tell you...

But of course, stories are why you're here! Well, brace yourself, because I have a hum-dum-dinger of a tale set to send your thoughts running for cover. A story so truly unbelievable that it must, unbelievably, be true.

Our story begins many moons ago in Haggard Hall – a great, looming shadow of a house far from anywhere. In this house there lived a boy. He was alone, with no one to care for him and only his wild imagination for company. Haggard Hall was as lonely as darkness and so the boy imagined he had a friend to keep him company. He named his IF Mumbo Jumbo, for a fantabulant friend – however imaginary – deserves a fantabulant name. Mumbo Jumbo was a marvellous magical man, chock-brimming with flabbergasting spells and tricks, and he made the boy feel altogether less alone.

Then, one fate-filled, moonish night the boy imagined his friend so wildly and so well

that something rather remarkable happened –
Mumbo Jumbo became as real as teeth!

The magical man's spells and tricks were
even more flabbergasting in real life, and all
he cared about was making the boy happier
than Christmas.

But the boy was not happy. You see, despite
the house being big enough for both of them
– big enough for a hundred Mumbo Jumbos
– the boy realized he did not like sharing it.
He did not like sharing the shadows and the
silence. He wanted to be alone again.

But once an IF is unimagined, he cannot
be un-unimagined – and so the boy banished
Mumbo Jumbo from Haggard Hall. The
marvellous magical man begged the boy to
let him stay but his pleas fell upon deaf ears.
At last, Mumbo Jumbo vanished in a puff of
sadness, and was gone.

In time, the boy grew into a man, and the

man into an old man. He had a family but still he did not learn to share. Every day, he would remind his own flesh and blood that he would much rather be alone.

I am sure you are cram-bursting at the seams to be introduced to the boy that became known as Old Man Moon! But alas, like a winged cow, it is impossible, for there is one thing I have not told you...

Old Man Moon is quite dead.

Only his granddaughter, Luna, is sorry to see him go. But perhaps the old man's story is not over yet. For strange things can happen when imaginations run wild...

Guy Bass is an award-winning author and
semi-professional geek. He has written over thirty books,
including the best-selling *Stitch Head* series (which has been
translated into sixteen languages) *Dinkin Dings and the
Frightening Things* (winner of a 2010 Blue Peter Book Award)
*Spynosaur, Laura Norder: Sheriff of Butts Canyon, Noah Scape
Can't Stop Repeating Himself, Atomic!* and *The Legend of Frog.*

Guy has previously written plays for both adults and children.
He lives in London with his wife and imaginary dog.
Find out more at guybass.com

Pete Williamson is a self-taught artist and illustrator. He is best known for the much-loved *Stitch Head* series by Guy Bass, and the award-winning *The Raven Mysteries* by Marcus Sedgwick.

Pete has illustrated over sixty-five books by authors including Francesca Simon, Matt Haig and Charles Dickens. Before that he worked as a designer in an animation company (while daydreaming about being a children's book illustrator).

Pete now lives in rural Kent with a big piano, a writer wife and a dancing daughter. Find out more at petewilliamson.co.uk

Have you read *Stitch Head*?

'It's dark, monstrous fun!' Wondrous Reads

In Castle Grotteskew something BIG
is about to happen to someone SMALL.
Join a mad professor's first creation as
he steps out of the shadows into the
adventure of an almost lifetime...

Read all Stitch Head's adventures:

The Pirate's Eye

The Ghost of Grotteskew

THE SPIDER'S LAIR

The Beast of Grubbers Nubbin

THE MONSTER HUNTER

BEHIND THE SCENES
OF SKELETON KEYS

Guy gives us the lowdown on the characters ... with some help from Pete's early sketches...

How did Skeleton Keys come to life?

The name came first ... then most of the bones, then the keys, then a few more bones. I liked the idea of a skeleton with keys for fingers, who lived in a dimension filled with an infinite number of doors. His keys could literally take him anywhere on earth and beyond.

Did you have a particular look in mind for Ben?

My description was fairly loose – I just wanted Ben
to have a bowl of black hair. Pete sent a few sketches
through and one of them just was Ben. It was exactly as I
imagined him.

And how did Daisy end up with a backwards head?

I had an action figure of a character from the Twilight Zone
TV show that had its leg put on the wrong way round, and
that gave me the idea for a girl with a backwards head. I
wanted her to look pretty unsettling at first glance. Not that
Daisy is bothered about her appearance – she's much more
worried about being forgotten.

And how did the Gorblimey evolve into such a friendly-looking monster?

I always imagined the Gorblimey as looking like a hairy, jet-black shadow but I originally saw him as a towering monster. Pete sent through a sketch showing Skeleton Keys, Ben and the Gorblimey side by side and the Gorblimey was smaller – only a little taller than Ben. Suddenly he was much more appealing, so I rewrote the story to match.

SKELETON KEYS WILL RETURN